The
Comics
Open

The Comics Open

Ron Kenney

SAMO PRESS, INC.
SANTA MONICA, CALIFORNIA

This book is a work of fiction. Names, characters, places and events are products of the author's imagination or are used fictitiously. Any resemblance to actual events, locations, or persons, living or deceased, is purely coincidental. We assume no responsibility for errors, inaccuracies, omissions, or any inconsistency herein.

First printing 2000

ISBN 0-9676671-5-1

LCCN 99-97567

Cover design by Eric M. Weiss, Raine Street Graphic Design Company

ATTENTION CORPORATIONS, UNIVERSITIES, COLLEGES, AND PROFESSIONAL ORGANIZATIONS: Quantity discounts are available on bulk purchases of this book for educational purposes. Special books or book excerpts can also be created to fit specific needs. For information, please contact Samo Press, Inc., 2436 Fourth Street, #7, Santa Monica, CA 90405.

I am proud to say that Ron Kenney is one of a group of younger comedians that I lecture on occasion. He is bright and funny and makes good use of my humble suggestions. My stock in him now rises, as he becomes an author.

His description of young comedians on stage and back stage both enlightened me as to today's show business and reminded me of my own wonderful early days.

He writes about golf in his story with the full passion I had in going from a bare beginner to an eight handicap.

The comedians getting ready to stage a golf tournament for charity is very funny and the story goes on to an O. Henry finish.

It is a good read, easy, light and very entertaining.

Buddy Hackett

DEDICATED TO

Dr. John P. Kenney, Ph.D.,
a great dad and a very funny golfer.

ACKNOWLEDGMENTS

I would like to thank some of the people who have read so much of my material over the years: Chuck Friedrichs, Andy Huggins, Uncle Jake Kenney, Sandy Hackett, Roger "Wilko" Wilkerson, and Jerry Edling.

CHAPTER ONE

If you were a comedian fifteen years ago you could get laid even if you had a wart on the end of your nose the size of a basketball. You could drink for free all week at the comedy club you were performing at and if you were into drugs, audiences members would fight over who got to get you high. Because you were considered so special, most of the laws and ordinances that applied to everyone else didn't really apply to you. The few people who were offended by your actions usually just murmured to themselves, "What the hell. They're moving on at the end of the week anyway."

I once heard comedians back then described as "tornadoes. They hit town with a lot of excitement and then everyone is glad to see them leave."

If you had fifteen to forty-five minutes' worth of jokes, you could tour the country playing comedy clubs. Every major city had a comedy club, as did many of the towns. Your job was to make people laugh and then party all night. And if you got up at all the next day, it was to go to a free lunch, movie, or complimentary round of golf. You would do that six days a week with Monday as your travel day.

At the free lunch that some restaurant owner or manager treated you to after seeing you at the local comedy club, you could act like an idiot and your behavior would not only be tolerated—it would be expected. Behavior that would get a paying patron thrown out of that same restaurant would get you a round of applause. As you were walking by someone's table on your way to be seated, you could stop and say, "Your iced tea doesn't look right." You could take a sip of that person's iced tea and then say, "No, it tastes okay. Go ahead and finish it. And don't let the sore on my lip bother you."

The restaurant owner or manager would then say with a wide smile to that customer and every other customer who saw the scene, "He's a comedian performing here in town."

"He's a comedian" or "they're comedians" would also get you out of trouble at the movie theater after you decided your lines were better or funnier than the actors on the screen were. If it was a horror movie then one of the comedians was probably screaming at the screen, "You idiot! Doesn't the scary music tell you the monster is behind that door you're about to open?"

A car chase scene would prompt a comic to yell, "That's me trying to get to the liquor store before it closes!" Then the comic would yell, "Oops!" as the car drove into a telephone pole.

The same people who complained about you in the theater wanted to meet you after the movie after being told that you were a real live comedian.

Even at private golf courses, it was the same deal. "Get that golf cart off the putting green!" The starter would scream through his microphone in the pro shop. That would get you thrown out of the country club and the person whose guest you were would probably lose his membership. But all would be smoothed over when the starter was informed you were a comedian performing at the local comedy club that week. You would tell him a couple of jokes after your round, invite him to the comedy club, and you would be the starter's guest for your round of golf on Sunday.

In theory, no one is allowed to fool around on airplanes—not even comedians. But back then comedians were getting away with taking the microphone away from the flight attendant and making announcements like, "Whoever buys me drinks all the way back to Houston will be comped into my show tomorrow night!"

I'll never forget my first "road gigs." I performed at a comedy club in Austin and then one the following week in Dallas. I had the opening spot on those shows where I would do fifteen minutes, then introduce the middle act, and then the headliner. Those were the two greatest weeks of my life to that point, and I was offered everything a twenty-one-year-old male could think of or even fantasize about.

My best memory of that week in Austin was of a young lady who I didn't know had a weekly habit of sleeping with a comic who happened to be passing through the local comedy club. I was the lucky one that week. When we woke up the next morning together I asked her a stupid question: "Have you ever done this before?"

She answered, "What? Sleep with the emcee? No, I usually just do middle acts and headliners."

My reaction was shock, to say the least, and then I remember saying something like, "Thanks for taking on a charity case."

I got to feel like a celebrity my first two weeks on the comedy road. One of the comics I worked with in Dallas summed it up pretty well when he said to me early one morning, "Right now being a comedian is kind of like the way it was being an astronaut. People have heard about them and maybe they've seen one on television but now they have a chance to go out and see one in their own town. We're like the astronauts and right now everybody wants to meet the astronauts."

Another thing that made my first two weeks on the comedy road so special was simply the fact that I got to get away from home. I loved my hometown of Houston, Texas, but like any young man I couldn't wait to get away to spread my wings, if only for two weeks. Out of town I could escape the almost constant scrutiny I felt in Houston. But out of town I could get arrested and in Houston I couldn't. In Houston, I was constantly aware that I didn't want to do anything to embarrass my father. Just being a comedian was pushing that envelope a little bit.

Dad and I were great friends and he was supportive of my career choice but I hated it when someone would use his name in my introduction. Every once in a while a comedy club emcee would forget my instructions and introduce me as, "Comedian Dale Chase! The son of Houston's chief of police, Bertram Chase!"

My dad had a lot to do with my going into comedy. We never stopped rehashing the night he introduced me to an audience of about three hundred people. I was twelve. Dad had to speak at a lot of dinners and sometimes he would take me along if my mom didn't feel like going or if he just felt like spending more time with me. As we rode to one of those dinners he said, "Why don't I introduce you tonight and you do your routine with all of your impressions? They'd love it. And don't forget to do Barney Fife."

I will remember that moment and the entire evening for the rest of my life. I felt like all of the electricity in Houston was charging through my body as I said, "Yes, I'll do it."

The dinner was in a high school gymnasium and we were sitting at the main table, which was below a stage at the end of the room. My dad was to speak at a podium and he told me he would lift me up to that stage and then hand me the microphone.

Toward the end of his speech my father said, "I would like to defer some of my time tonight to introduce you to my twelve-year-old son who has turned into a fine little entertainer." He lifted me up to the stage and, before he handed me the microphone, said, "Ladies and gentlemen, Dale Chase."

There was a nice round of applause and I stared out over the audience, probably looking like a deer stuck in headlights. It was surreal. I had never even held a microphone before but I finally said into it, "Ladies and gentlemen, my impression of the chief of police, Bertram Chase." I did my impression of his walk, which got a little laughter, and then I did my dad's two favorite slogans, for which he was famous. My voice was too high to do his correctly but I certainly had his voice pattern down as I said, "Houstonians looking out for each other is the greatest police work." And, "Drugs have the potential to destroy this city from the inside out." The audience laughed and gave me another round of applause, probably out of respect for my dad.

I then went into a routine I had down pat, a series of celebrities giving safety tips. I did Johnny Carson, Edith and Archie Bunker, Redd Foxx, and Kermit the Frog, giving advice like, "Wear white at night," and "Walk facing the traffic." The audience seemed to laugh harder and applaud more with each impression.

I closed with my dad's favorite impression, which was Don Knotts as Barney Fife on *The Andy Griffith Show* saying, "Drink and drive and you'll hear the big door slam." The audience gave me a tremendous ovation. As I was basking in the glory, I looked down at my dad, who was beaming up at me. We both knew right then in what direction my life would go.

It was all we talked about on the ride home. Then suddenly my dad did something I will also never forget. He pulled the car over in front of two men who were standing on a street corner. He got out and introduced himself. The men already knew who he was. Without even pulling out a gun, my dad told them to empty the contents of their pockets on to the hood of the car. They slowly pulled out some Baggies and small amounts of cash. My dad picked up the Baggies and told the men, "Pick up your money. Now, get out of here."

On the drive home Dad showed me the Baggies and described what drugs were in each and what kind of an effect the drug would have on a person. He pulled the car over to the curb and said, "These are illegal drugs. You doing these is out of the question. You'll make your own decision on the legal drugs of alcohol and tobacco." He then had me open the car door and throw the Baggies down a storm drain.

Even more than seeing drugs for the first time was why my father didn't arrest those men and why he let them keep their money.

He answered my questions this way: "First of all," he began, "it wouldn't have been a legal arrest. They weren't doing anything illegal; they were just standing there. But I knew they were drug dealers and I wanted to show you what the drugs look like, plus do a little police work. I couldn't have taken their money because what would I have done with it? I couldn't keep it and I couldn't turn it in because there wasn't an arrest. Dale, what happened was some street justice and a little tradeoff. They lost the drugs and they hated that, but they weren't arrested and they got to keep their money. Sometimes justice is a tradeoff."

My heart had pounded harder watching my dad face those two men than it did when I faced that audience of three hundred. I had heard that a comedian could "die onstage," but I knew that was just an expression. A cop dying in the street was a reality. I was frozen in fear as I watched my father confront those drug dealers. He looked like a toreador with his perfect posture as he faced down not one, but two, dangerous bulls. It was at that moment as I watched the scene play out in front of me in the headlights of my father's car that I made my lifelong career decision. I was going to take the easier, softer way—I was going into standup comedy.

CHAPTER TWO

I had just finished my parents' last requirement of me, which was graduating from college, when I did my first out-of-town gigs. They knew where I was going when I graduated. I was going into comedy full time, which was what I had been doing almost every night my last three years at the University of Houston. I was performing and hanging out at Milt and Marty's comedy club. As far as I was concerned, Milt and Marty's comedy club was the center of the universe.

Milt and Marty were brothers but they certainly didn't look like it. Marty looked like one of the Kennedy brothers and Milt looked like one of The Marx Brothers. Marty was a leading man type and I overheard two girls debating once whether he looked more like Paul Newman or Robert Redford. He did in fact look like a cross between Butch Cassidy and the Sundance Kid. Milt looked like a cross between Beavis and Butthead.

Milt was born with spina bifida, rendering him paralyzed from the waist down. He was put into his first wheelchair when he was two years old. Marty learned to walk by pulling himself up on that wheelchair and then taking his first steps as Milt cheered him on. That's how

Marty developed such strong legs and became what Milt described as "one fine white running back." Marty parlayed those running skills into a full-ride scholarship to Rice University in Houston.

Milt thought a lot and Marty had a business degree. Milt had ideas and Marty could figure out what those ideas would cost. Milt was the dreamer and Marty thought it was his job to make Milt's dreams come true.

They would have made a pretty good comedy team if Marty had it in him to go onstage. It only happened once and I got to see it at about three in the morning after their comedy club had closed. Marty had drunk just enough "foam courage" and the audience in the show room was just a bunch of us comedians and other friends. Marty pushed Milt in his wheelchair up on to the stage and they were going to try to do the classic Abbott and Costello comedy routine, "Who's On First?"

Marty had memorized the routine and gone over it many times with his brother while in their car. Milt could not wait to get Marty onstage to do the routine and then completely screw up his anal-retentive brother.

Marty started it off doing Abbott's part, explaining how some baseball players have strange names. They then started working their way through the routine and the infield: "Who's on first. What's on second and I Don't Know is on third."

Milt waited for what he thought was the perfect moment and threw his brother a big curve ball by saying, "You don't know shit."

We in the audience were shocked at what Milt did and held our collective breath as we waited for Marty's reaction. Marty handled Milt's curve ball perfectly by saying, "I do too know Shit. Shit is the umpire."

The audience roared and we wildly applauded Marty. Milt came back with, "Screw you."

Marty didn't miss a beat as he said, "Screw You is the Chinese shortstop."

The audience roared again and Milt tried, "Fuck you."

"Fuck You is Screw You's brother," answered Marty. "But he's still in the minor leagues."

Milt was as amazed as we were that Marty could ad-lib so well. Marty seemed to get stronger and more confident each time. Milt tried again. "Blow job."

Marty appeared stuck for the first time and he looked to the ceiling as if the answer was printed there. He then got the expression anyone gets when they finally remember the name they were trying to think of. Marty said, "Blow Job works in the front office and she's a big hit in the locker room."

"Known homosexual."

"Known Homosexual also works in the front office but he's not allowed in the locker room."

"Dick head," said Milt with tears of laughter rolling down his face.

Marty answered, "Dick Head is the owner of the team."

Milt's last try was, "Butt hole."

"Butt Hole is the team mascot," Marty answered. "I'll buy you a miniature stuffed Butt Hole at the souvenir stand after the game."

It was a great moment and Milt and Marty slapped hands onstage as we in the crowd cheered wildly. It was the one and only time I ever saw Marty onstage let alone performing comedy. Marty was smart and he knew he was no comedian. He explained it to me one night: "I tried it once and I got away with it. You comedians do it every night and some nights it goes great and some nights it doesn't. But I got to have my moment. I got to have a little taste and I'll just quit while I'm ahead."

Marty was the only one smart enough to even consider that the comedy club phenomenon might not last forever. In fact, it didn't. Ten years later, there were half as many comedy clubs in the country as there were back then and less that half as much work for the comedians whose numbers seemed to have doubled.

Marty feared even then that the comedy gravy train might end. He thought it possible the comedy clubs would be considered a fad and die the same death the discos did. Some strange music by groups with names like The Bee Gees and a movie called *Saturday Night Fever* starring John Travolta launched a new kind of night club called a "disco." Discos and disco music were going strong, and then one day someone yelled, "Disco sucks!" And disco died leaving clothing store owners stuck with thousands of pairs of bell-bottom pants and fabric traders wondering what happened to the polyester market.

Meanwhile, Milt was having too much fun and enjoying their success too well to hear that things could potentially go south. As he told me once, "It's Marty's job to worry. That's what he does best."

I offered, "I don't know, but Marty is usually right about stuff like this. Nothing lasts forever."

"Comedy is like rock-and-roll," Milt countered. "And rock-and-roll is here to stay. Comedy is not going to die so why should comedy clubs? This thing is too big and too popular. It's virtually indestructible."

"Sounds like you're describing the *Titanic*," I said. I could tell that line got Milt's attention.

Milt started to become more concerned, especially after one weekend when both Saturday night shows weren't sold out for just about the first time in their history.

Milt and Marty started discussing ways to get people to think of their club as more than just a business. They started sponsoring charity fund-raisers in their show room and I was on a lot of those shows. They even sponsored a Little League baseball team, although they lost that sponsorship when some of the comics showed up one Saturday morning at a game and taught the team a controversial cheer: "Boom! Boom! Hey! Hey! Our team's straight and your team's gay!"

I'll never forget the night Milt and Marty told me they wanted their comedy club to "stand the test of time" and "be a cornerstone of the community the way an opera house or playhouse was."

I was never sure why Milt and Marty respected my opinion or why they solicited it so much. I think it probably had a lot to do with the family I came from or, more specifically, my dad being the police chief. I told them they had delusions of grandeur if they thought their comedy club could be anything like an opera house or a playhouse. I explained, "Stand up comedy isn't like opera or the theater. Stand up comedy's roots are in burlesque. Opera house? Playhouse? The only house a comedy club is like is a whorehouse. At an opera the night is over when the fat lady sings. At a comedy club the night is over when the fat lady goes home with the comics."

But Milt and Marty were always trying to buy themselves some good will and were always thinking of ways to solidify comedy and the name of their club, The Comedy Werks, into the minds of the people of Houston. They thought they finally had it with the idea for The Comics Open.

The Comics Open was one of the biggest messes that ever happened and any good that came out of it could only be described as an accident. The hearts of the organizers and participants of The Open were in the right place but their egos and jealousies almost caused it to be called The Comics Disaster.

The thing that will always amaze me the most about The Open was how organized it *appeared* to be. It had a board of directors, sponsors, and even a press conference to announce when the whole thing was going to happen. To me, that was like saying a natural disaster had a board of directors and "this hurricane is brought to you by Spartan Sportswear. Don't be caught in a storm in anything less than Spartan Sportswear." And the press conference was no different to me than saying, "There is going to be a citywide riot Monday but it's okay because all the proceeds will go to charity."

I hate to say it, but The Comics Open came very close to killing comedy in Houston. It was a miracle that only one person went to jail. I know *I* came pretty close to jail myself and almost caused a lot of embarrassment to my dad and his department. I'll always wonder why I got so involved and so caught up in the insanity. If I would have had to go to court then I would have pleaded, "Temporary insanity, brought on by overexposure to comedians."

I don't have anyone to blame but myself because the whole thing just happened to be my idea. There were times I cussed that particular night I wandered into The Comedy Werks. I figured if I had just gone home like I was supposed to, the idea never would have come to me.

CHAPTER THREE

The Comics Open had its genesis at three o'clock on a March morning, and I pointed as I said, "Looks like another alcohol-related accident."

I studied the wreckage and the body lying beneath it. Through the spokes of one of the wheels I could see that the body was laughing and its eyes were squinting from the stage lights overhead. I smiled at the man on the ground and said, "You okay, Milt?"

A voice weak with laughter came back from beneath the heap of metal, "Get this thing off of me, Dale, and lift me up. The other guys think it's funny to leave me laying here with this thing on top of me."

I said to no one in particular, "Another casualty of the wheelchair races."

There were twelve or so comedians, girlfriends, and hangers-on standing at the bar laughing at the situation. As I picked up Milt and started to put him back in his wheelchair, someone from the bar yelled, "The Chief's Kid to the rescue!"

Most of the comics in Houston had nicknames and mine of course was "The Chief's Kid." Either that or

"Opie." I did look a little bit like Andy Griffith's TV son, Opie, who was played by Ron Howard. I was just under six feet with hair closer to red than brown. I had a few freckles on and around my nose, which prompted one of the comedians to say, "He looks like Tom Sawyer and Jane Fonda had a kid."

A black comedian and part-time bartender by the name of Brent Harris once described me as, "an average-looking white boy with a halfway decent jump shot." I thought that summed me up pretty well, and I did in fact have a halfway decent jump shot I displayed during the comedians' pickup basketball games.

Brent yelled to me from behind the bar, "Hey, Dale! Tell your dad I don't care how he does it but he has to keep the Negroes under control!"

As I went down the bar and slapped hands with the comics, each one of them had a comment. Fred Huggins said to me, "Ladies and gentlemen, it's the undercover comedy of Dale Chase."

The comic standing next to Fred blurted out, "He calls his daddy 'Chief' and he's no friggin' Indian—Dale Chase!"

The next comic yelled, "*My Pop the Cop*! A new sitcom on CBS this fall! Watch as the wisecracking son of the chief of police asks his father, 'Pop, can I have the keys to the storage area at the police department where the confiscated drugs are stored? I want to show my classmates what to keep their eyes out for.'"

Comedians never said "Hello." They would just make some comment in an effort to write the correct caption. You are just a picture to a comedian and they feel it is their job to come up with the right caption when they see you. I wore a Hawaiian shirt into the club one night, which prompted one of the comics to say, "Nice shirt. Did Don Ho have a garage sale?"

An oversized sweatshirt would draw a comment like, "What an interesting wardrobe choice—a car cover."

I was standing next to a comic one night as we watched an incredibly good-looking young lady enter the club by herself and walk up to the bar and order a beer. The comic never took his eyes off that young lady as he said under his breath, "The mysterious woman enters the comedy club after a long day of breaking hearts. She orders a beer and contemplates crushing the heart of one of the comics before she calls it a day and goes home alone."

That was how I ended up getting some of my best material. I was a very good impressionist but a mediocre joke writer, so I would use the comedians' comments about me to strengthen my act. They gave me jokes about my dad being chief like, "Dad was responsible for my first time onstage. It was just like this. Bright lights, people staring at me. It was a police lineup." Another one was, "For my ninth birthday my dad gave me a fully grown German shepherd police dog named 'Kill.' Every time I would call the dog he would attack me."

The after-hours drinking and partying in Milt and Marty's club was probably as important as the performing of the standup comedy during business hours. Cops hang out at cop bars and gays hang out at gay bars for the same reasons comics hung out at The Comedy Werks after-hours. People love to socialize with people who understand what they are going through. Only the comedians understood each other's fears and anxieties.

Marty handed me a beer from behind the bar and I said "Hi" to the waitress Patty. Then I asked the waitress Carolyn how her new boyfriend Jim Peters was. He was a human-interest reporter on one of the local television news stations. But before Carolyn could answer, the comedians started in. Harry Bosco pretended to use his long-neck beer bottle as a microphone as he said, "And now let's go to the state fair, where Jim Peters is standing with a man who has grown a watermelon in the same size and shape as actor Marlon Brando."

The comedian standing next to Harry yelled into his beer bottle, "Sex for sale! For the past month our own investigative reporter Jim Peters has been frequenting titty bars and massage parlors to expose sex for sale in Houston. We will have Jim's report just as soon as we can wipe the smile off his face."

Carolyn and I just laughed and then I had to take my beer off the bar because two of the comic's girlfriends started to do a go-go dance on the bar as the song "Disco Inferno" pounded through the sound system.

Milt had organized another wheelchair race with his best wheelchair-bound friend, Art Harold. The tiny strawberry blond waitress Carolyn was to ride on Art's lap and the big-busted waitress Patty was to ride on Milt's. Harry Bosco and his girlfriend were to race in a third wheelchair Milt kept around for just that reason.

All of the tables and chairs were piled in the middle of the show room. The racecourse started at the back bar and went along the back wall, then took a big sweeping left turn, up the ramp onto the stage, and then down the other side. It continued with a big sweeping turn past the bathrooms, the office, the comic's green room, and then back to the bar. The entire club was ramped for Milt and was greatly supported by the wheelchair community of Houston because it was so accessible.

As the race started I yelled to Marty, "It looks like the chariot race scene in the movie *Ben-Hur!*"

Harry Bosco and his girlfriend crashed in turn one on the first lap and were both thrown from their wheelchair. They never even tried to get back up and into the race. They just made out on the floor as the other two teams navigated around them.

The team of Art Harold and Carolyn won the wheel-chair race when Patty and Milt missed the ramp on the down side and ended up on the floor. Carolyn and Art might have won the race but no one was laughing harder then Patty, Milt, and even Marty.

I had met Milt and Marty at a civic pride dinner where I was to do some of my act. I did a lot of dinners like that and I was especially good with high school kids and the Boys and Girls Clubs around the city. I liked it because it gave me stage experience and I knew my dad liked me to do it.

I did well at that dinner and the highlight of my performance was my impression of Mick Jagger singing "Take Me Out to the Ballgame" during the seventh-inning stretch at the Astrodome during a Houston Astros baseball game.

My finale also went over well when I said, "If my dad was here tonight he would probably say," (I then went into my impression of George C. Scott as General George Patton) "'Houston loves a winner and will not tolerate a loser. I wouldn't give a hoot in hell for a man whose store was looted and he laughed.'"

Milt was introduced after me and I'll never forget his opening statement. "Ladies and gentlemen, it's nice to be here. There has been a big move lately to have handi-capped people speak at these kinds of functions. I'm just filling in for a blind guy who got lost tonight. But I think I will be speaking at a lot of these dinners because I have an inspirational story, and as you can see, I have my own transportation."

The audience loved it as they did his next bit. "You know, there were never any role models on television for me growing up except for the show *Ironside*. And I don't believe that the actor who played Ironside, Raymond Burr, was really paralyzed from the waist down. I think he just got too fat to walk so he bought himself a wheelchair and hired that black guy to push him around."

For his finale he said, "Ladies and gentlemen, my impression of a wheelchair wagon train heading west." He then went over to the side of the stage where he had come up a ramp and there seven members of his wheel-chair basketball team joined him in single file and as they went slowly across the stage they said things like, "Is this the way to Yuma?" "How far to the next watering hole?" "Are those smoke signals?" "What kind of Indians would attack a bunch of cripples?"

I introduced myself to Milt and Marty that night and we really hit it off. They said that they had liked my show and the only thing they said that made me happier than that statement was their answer to my question, "Can I perform at your club when I graduate from college?"

Marty answered, "Why wait until after college?" Milt added, "Start hanging out and performing at our club now."

I was ecstatic to be accepted by Milt and Marty but I was shocked to find that the comedians were an entirely different matter. When I first went to The Comedy Werks I was accepted about as well as a fart in church. It didn't have as much to do with me as it did with my dad. Patty the waitress explained it to me one night: "The comics think of you the same way they think of the son of the chaperone on prom night. They just figure you are a spy."

I solved the problem late one Saturday night when I invited the core group of the comedians at The Comedy Werks out to the back parking lot. They thought I was inviting them out to fight but when the dozen or so of us got to the parking lot I asked if any of them had a mari-juana cigarette. One of the comics handed me a joint and, although I don't smoke marijuana, I lit it up and took two puffs off it. The other comics were bug-eyed as I handed the joint back to the comic who gave it to me and said, "There you go. Now you've got the goods on me. You can all say you watched the son of the chief smoke a joint in the parking lot of The Comedy Werks."

Everything settled down after that incident and no one mentioned my dad again except for two comics who weren't even from Houston. They were two guys from Fort Worth and I finally got tired of them busting my balls. I had a friend in the police department do a background check on both of them. It was the wrong thing to do and I know my dad wouldn't have liked it, but I enjoyed confronting them alone one night in front of The Comedy Werks. I asked one guy, "Why don't you go back to Fort Worth and start paying your child support?" I told the other one, "You ought to leave too and not come back until you get all of your warrants taken care of."

I never saw those two after that and no one ever mentioned them so I tried to rationalize that I had done everyone a favor. It was the first time I ever played cop but it wouldn't be the last. The last time I did it was during The Comics Open.

It was during the last lap of the wheelchair race that the man appeared who gave me the idea for The Comics Open. Houston's pride and joy, touring PGA golfer Bobby Ray Sutton, walked into the show room wearing the same clothes and hat he had worn in the qualifying round that day at a tournament in Dallas. He was barefoot except for his sweat socks and he had his bag of clubs slung over his left shoulder. He had a beer in his right hand and appeared fairly drunk and very depressed.

When the music ended and everyone finally stopped laughing at the result of the wheelchair race, their attention turned to Bobby Ray. Bobby Ray's first words were, "Marty, you're my best friend and since I didn't make the cut today for the fifth tournament in a row I've lost my touring card. And since I'm quitting golf, I just stopped by to give you my most prized possessions: my golf bag and clubs."

Everyone in the show room rushed to Bobby Ray's rescue.

"You're just in a slump," said one of the comics.

"Yeah," said Marty as he walked around from behind the bar. "And it's only going to make you stronger when you snap out of it."

Someone hollered, "Houstonians don't quit!"

"I've seen you play on television!" yelled Brent Harris.

Harry Bosco's girlfriend was just drunk enough to offer, "Bobby Ray, me and most of the girls in Houston think you've got the nicest butt on the PGA Tour."

Fred Huggins took Bobby Ray's clubs from him, and Carolyn approached him with a fresh beer and handed it to him as she said shyly, "You can't quit. You're my hero."

Marty got Bobby Ray up on the stage and got him to start swinging a club, as if a drunken comedy club owner, ten drunken comedians, and two drunk waitresses were going to help a drunk golf pro with his golf swing. But it was good therapy for Bobby Ray. He enjoyed being onstage and showing everyone the proper grip, stance, and fundamentals of the swing.

Bobby Ray then went out to his car and brought in a huge sack of plastic golf balls, the kind with little holes in them. From the stage, he started hitting them around the show room. He took out a wedge and started lofting balls from the stage, to just over the bar, to the applause of his audience. He then took out a seven iron and hit balls into the liquor bottles on the top shelf behind the bar and then the shelf just beneath it, as his audience cheered. He took out a fairway wood and again called his shot and sliced it down the hallway and hit the door of the dressing room on a fly.

Soon Bobby Ray had completely forgotten about his problems. He handed out clubs and began teaching everyone in the show room how to swing them. He especially enjoyed standing behind big-busted Patty, as he reached around her while he taught her how to grip a club.

I was enjoying watching it all with my beer at the bar. I noticed that Milt and Art figured out if they took the right sides of their wheelchairs off—the piece where the armrest was—they could swing golf clubs. They then figured out if they took the left armrest off too, they could swing a club and follow through as well as anybody. Milt also found out that if he overswung and followed through too far, he would fall out of his chair.

By four-twenty that morning, so many golf balls were flying around the show room it looked like a hailstorm. The only accident happened when comedian Jimmy Clark got hit in the face with a golf club and it broke his nose. Milt said the accident was divine intervention because Jimmy had become a little too fond of cocaine. Milt explained, "A broken nose will keep him from snorting that shit for at least a month."

It was about four-thirty when I got the basic idea for The Comics Open. I ran it over a couple of times in my head to see if it still made sense and it seemed that it did. Golf had become a popular game with many of the comics, because their days were always free. It didn't matter whether they could play or not, since the tournament was to be for entertainment. That many comics playing golf had to be hysterical. A show with that many comics performing at the banquet would have to be a classic. I got Milt and Marty's attention and gestured for them to follow me over to a table in a quiet corner.

When Milt and Marty sat down at the table next to me, I shared my idea. "A comedian's golf tournament," I said. "The Comics Open. It's a natural. There are always celebrity and pro golf tournaments around the country that raise money for charities. Comedians could come from all over and you could use Bobby Ray Sutton as the golf pro. He could help us get a course at a country club and sponsors would line up to get involved. All of the comedians would receive prizes like shirts and sweaters and all of the money would go to Houston charities. And it would get you guys the positive publicity you've been looking for."

No one spoke. I was beginning to think they hated my idea until Milt looked directly at his brother and said, "This could be the thing that we've always talked about. This could be the thing that legitimizes comedy in Houston and solidifies the name 'The Comedy Werks' into the hearts and minds of the people of Houston."

Marty didn't speak and I could tell he was in deep thought. A plastic golf ball came whizzing by our table and nobody even flinched.

Milt obviously loved the idea and he wanted his brother to as well. He looked at me and added, "And we can get the police department behind it, can't we, Dale?"

I said calmly, "I'll start working on my dad now and he'll be a major supporter of The Comics Open before he even knows it."

Milt smiled excitedly and said, "The whole thing is a natural where everybody wins. And who knows how big it will get?"

There was a long pause and Marty, always the more conservative of the two, spoke, "You're right. It's a natural. It's a sure thing—absolutely everyone involved wins. And the idea of filming or taping the show at the banquet and part of the comics on the golf course could make a ton of money for us and the comedians if we can sell it to television."

He thought a while longer and he started to look doubtful. He added, "I always think of the best-case scenario and the worst-case scenario. And the worst-case scenario for this thing would be that it could get too big for us and get out of control. Charities could be promised money they don't get and sponsors could end up getting disappointed or pissed off. And who knows how the comics are going to act at this thing. They could gross out the entire city, including TV and radio, and that could ruin us."

Milt's snap answer was, "You're right Marty, but we can control the whole thing. It will work because, like you said, everybody wins. We have connections and you're a great organizer and you know how to use Bobby Ray and control him."

What Milt said next we all agreed later was the dumbest line in the history of mankind. What he said next was, "And don't worry about the comedians. I can control the comedians."

CHAPTER FOUR

The news of the rumored golf tournament and show spread like wildfire through the comedy community of Houston. Milt could not figure out how everyone found out about it so fast. "The only person I told about it was Clay," he said. Deveraux Clay Clayton was the class of all the comedians in Houston, onstage and off.

I explained to Milt his mistake: "If you told one comedian then you have told them all."

Marty added, "The comedians are a runaway train of bad ideas."

Milt looked bewildered. Marty's expression reminded me of someone who was driving downhill and just realized his brakes don't work. I don't know what my face looked like, but I was getting the feeling in the pit of my stomach that always meant something bad was going to happen.

None of us—Milt, Marty, or myself—was about to admit it but The Comics Open was already out of control and it was barely in the planning stages.

The three of us were in a frenzy as we tried to regain control of the tournament. When Clay started the snowball rolling by telling the comedians about the proposed golf tournament, they all felt they had a great idea for it. Too many comedians and comedy club personnel had too many different ideas on what the tournament was supposed to be and what was supposed to happen at it.

"Live bands on the golf course! Have you heard that one, Marty?" Milt asked his brother one night in their office. "Now they want to make it a golf tournament/rock concert!"

"There has to be some structure and some rules," said Marty adamantly.

"Yeah," Milt concurred and then he looked at me and said, "Dale, I was smart. I knew what I wanted—I wanted a comedy club. And I was smart enough to know that I couldn't have one without Marty. The comedians aren't smart that way—the worst people I can think of to own and run a comedy club are comedians. It's the same with the tournament. The tournament has to be for the comedians, but the comedians can't have anything to do with running it. They are performers. They are to play in the tournament and perform at the banquet, but their involvement in any planning or running of the tournament would be a disaster."

For the sake of the tournament, Milt and Marty knew they couldn't relinquish any control. If I was on their team, that would ruin my reputation with the comedians. I was to be involved behind the scenes and help protect my interests indirectly. I certainly had a stake in how the tournament turned out because I had already gotten my dad and his department involved.

I had told my dad about The Comics Open and how we could use the backing of the chief of police and his department. He went along with it and ordered a small press conference to announce his support of The Comics Open at the police department where we had our picture taken with Milt and Marty. That picture and the one the four of us took onstage at The Comedy Werks both made the papers. While we were having our picture taken at The Comedy Werks, I whispered to my dad, "Don't tell any jokes." I should have listened harder to him when he whispered back, "Don't embarrass me and I won't embarrass you."

Milt and Marty spent a lot of time coming up with rules, regulations, and guidelines. They even came up with a board of directors for the tournament, which was the two of them and golf pro Bobby Ray Sutton. I suggested they have a woman on the board and they settled on Brenda Brookshire, who had been a Comedy Werks waitress and was now a three-year touring comedienne. Marty was to control Bobby Ray, and Milt was to control Brenda.

We had to have Bobby Ray because he was a celebrity around Houston and he could help secure a country club for us. He would attract potential sponsors, plus it looked good to have a touring PGA pro on the board of directors. Milt and Marty liked my idea of having a woman on the board. They picked Brenda because she was a comic, which would make the comedians happy, and it was rumored she was a fine golfer.

Brenda was absolutely honored to be on the board of directors. She went right along with Milt and Marty when they laid out all of their rules and regulations at the first board of directors meeting and then the second. Those meetings were nothing more than Milt and Marty telling Brenda and Bobby Ray how it was going to be. Brenda just kept smiling and nodding her head. Bobby Ray really didn't care as long as he got to be the star. The third meeting was to be with all of the comics and comedy club personnel around Houston and at that meeting Milt and Marty were planning on laying down the law.

They picked a Sunday at noon to hold that meeting because they figured not too many people would attend. Comedians and comedy club personnel were known to sleep late, especially on Sundays, the day after the busiest party night of the week. Milt and Marty didn't want a lot of people there or any opposition as they pushed their rules and regulations through for The Comics Open.

Milt and Marty figured wrong. They were surprised to see a parade of comics as well as comedy club managers, bartenders, waitresses, and doormen in the show room of The Comedy Werks at noon that Sunday. Even former titty bar owner turned comedy club owner Hank Bruno was there. Hank was owner of The Comedy Corral on the west side of town. It was interesting that Hank was there because he didn't like comedians and none of the comedians liked him. Hank sat next to the stage with his girlfriend and away from most of the comics. Hank had a love-hate relationship with comedy. He loved the money his comedy club made him but hated comedians.

All told, about a hundred comics and comedy club personnel were in the show room and the bar or stood in the back of the room. The comics greeted me with their usual comments like, "Hey, Dale! Can your dad fix parking tickets? I parked my car on a homeless guy who was passed out on a bus bench."

Fred Huggins, Harry Bosco and Steven Reed (the house emcee at The Laff Trap in Austin) were standing together, and as I walked by Fred said, "It's Dale Chase starring in his autobiographical made-for-TV movie, *Cop or Comic?*"

Harry added, "In the climactic scene he confronts his father and with tears streaming down his cheeks he blubbers, 'But dad. I don't want to arrest people . . . I want to make them laugh.'"

Steven Reed said, "'Then you'll do neither,' his father the chief says as he produces a revolver and shoots Dale in the heart."

As I walked toward the back bar, Brent the bartender yelled loud enough for everyone to hear, "It's the chief's bag man! Hey, Dale! Tell your dad we don't have his shakedown money! We had a slow weekend! We need more time!"

I was wearing a golf shirt and a pair of shorts. Four comedy club waitresses and a couple of the comics' girlfriends jokingly commented on what great legs I had. So did Larry Lawrence but I didn't think he was kidding.

Larry Lawrence was an openly gay comic who was excellent at working with an audience. He would point out someone in the audience and then make fun of their clothes or their hair. One night he said to a man in the front row, "Sir, what scares me is not this frightening outfit you are wearing. I look at it and think, he picked this over something else, so what could his other clothes look like? Your closet must be a chamber of horrors. Speaking of closets—I'm out!"

One night Milt said of Larry, "Larry is so light in the loafers I'm afraid he is just going to float away."

Marty added, "Either that or burst into flames."

I introduced Larry to my dad one night and he said, "Nice to meet you, Chief. Is that a pistol in your pocket or are you just glad to see me?"

Larry's idea for The Comics Open was, "I see the comedians all wearing matching outfits. A hot pink or a dark purple depending on the time of the year the tournament is held."

The waitresses Patty and Carolyn approached me and they weren't smiling. Patty said, "Dale, I'm no psychic but I have a vision of the front page of one of the Houston newspapers. I can't see the headline but there is a picture of three golf carts floating in a lake. The picture on the lower half of the front page is of two paramedics trying to dislodge a golf ball from the forehead of a spectator."

Carolyn added, "A comedians golf tournament? Dale, comedians are no good outdoors."

Bobby Sanchez walked over to me and said, "Hey, Dale. I heard a rumor that we're finally going to be doing something I'm the best at."

"It looks like it, Super Mex," I answered. Bobby had been given Lee Trevino's nickname because he was Mexican and a super golfer. He had also been a best friend with Brenda Brookshire since high school and they had spent many hours together as he taught her the game of golf. "I taught her golf and she taught me how to dance," he once told me. "She invited me to the senior prom and instead of a corsage I gave her a new putter."

We had all rooted hard for Bobby when he first came to The Comedy Werks because he was such a nice guy, but he couldn't buy a laugh. His analogy was always, "Comedy is like hitting golf balls on a driving range. You shank a lot of them until you hit one sweet and there is no feeling like hitting a golf ball just right." Bobby once described his first year at The Comedy Werks as "a year-long shank."

Everyone at The Comedy Werks remembered the Monday night that "Bobby finally hit one sweet" and told his first good joke. "I have an uncle who is half Polish and half Mexican and he keeps sneaking over the border back into Mexico."

Marcus Pauley saw me and as usual threw his fist in the air and yelled, "Black power!"

I, as usual, responded by putting my fist in the air and yelling, "Police power!" We then slapped hands and Marcus told me, "Dale, I want you to be the first one to know. I'm gonna knock out the first one of these white boys who asks me to be his caddy in the golf tournament."

Brent said to Marcus from behind the bar, "Why can't we pick some game I know how to play? Why can't we have The Comics Basketball Tournament?"

Marcus laughed and said, "If you want to do the stereotypes then why don't we have a barbecue cooking contest? While you're cooking, I'll steal the stereos out of the white people's cars."

Marcus Pauley was a little over six feet tall with a good build and he looked menacing with his goatee. His act was "the angry young black man" who trashed the Bush administration, the state of Texas, and white people in general, and what laughs he did get could only be described as "laughter through intimidation." Offstage Marcus was completely the opposite of his stage character. Onstage, Marcus never smiled and offstage he was never without a smile.

As I walked along the bar I patted Greg Okada on the back and as he turned and saw me he said, "Pearl Harbor!" Greg usually greeted me that way because one night during our first year at The Comedy Werks we had an audience from hell and both Greg and I died onstage. Greg described our performances that night by saying, "Last time there was bombing like that my relatives were flying over Pearl Harbor."

Greg was a fine actor who had done two movies filmed in Houston as well as numerous television shows and commercials. He liked to team up with Brent Harris and Bobby Sanchez in an improvisational group and they did sketches about their three different ethnic backgrounds. They called the group "The Three Shades."

As I continued down the bar, Greg continued telling Brent, "I think it should be like field hockey. I think we should all wear helmets and all tee off at once and just hit balls into each other until someone is seriously injured."

Brent responded excitedly to that as he said, "Yeah! And we'll name it The Comics Combat Golf Tournament!"

Mike "Lurch" Raley, the bouncer at Jokesters Comedy Club was sitting next to Greg. No one ever told Mike to his face that he was too ugly and scary looking to do standup comedy. The club owner always let him go on last on the weeknight shows to drive the remaining audience members out so they could close up. Mike's idea for The Open was "should be more like polo. Two comics to a golf cart and you don't even slow down to hit the ball with your club."

"All of the above," said another one of the comics as I started to walk toward Milt and Marty's office. "We do it all at the Astrodome," he continued. "They'll let us use it because it's for charity. Fifty thousand people will buy tickets to watch Houston's comedians play baseball golf, hockey golf, polo golf. They'll pay to watch the mayhem. People will pay money to watch other people get hurt." I was shaking my head as I tried to figure out why that idea wouldn't work.

As I entered their office, both Milt and Marty were sitting behind their desk listening to four comics who were standing in front of them. I stood behind the four and watched as Alex Day said, "I agree that the name of the tournament should be The Comics Open but there should be a little something over it." Alex used his fingers to make the "quotes" sign as he continued, "In quotes and then with an exclamation mark at the end it should say, 'Everybody Duck!' and then, 'The Comics Open.' And the mascot will be a guy in a duck suit with a golf club through his head. He'll be like that San Diego Chicken mascot. I think I know where we can get a duck suit. We can get a lot of mileage out of that."

Milt was trying to be nice but he answered firmly, "Alex, I want to keep it simple. The Comics Open and the comedians are the mascots. That way we will have hundreds of mascots."

Marty looked at me and then Milt as he smiled and said, "From Birdies and Pars to Hardie Har Hars, It's The Comics Open."

"Alex has the right idea but the wrong slogan," offered Steven Reed. "Over 'The Comics Open' it should say 'Put It in the Hole!' And you have a caricature logo of a beautiful, big-busted girl who is tending the pin and pointing toward the hole as a golfer is trying to putt out. That slogan will get the attention of everybody in Houston."

Milt was shaking his head as he said to Steven, "No sexual innuendo stuff."

"Then I guess you'll hate my idea," said Fred Huggins. "Milt, the top golf tournament in the country is The Masters. And since all of the comics in Houston are thought of as bunch of jerkoffs, we'll call our tournament 'The Master Baters.'"

It was a silly joke and Marty and I were barely laughing at it but we loved Milt's response as he said sarcastically, "Yeah, and our logo will be a caricature of a comedian with a microphone in one hand and his dick in the other."

The conversation started to bottom out as Monte Miller said in mock seriousness as he started to pitch his idea, "I think it's called an acronym. The first letter of each word spells out a message. I think the name should be Comics Open Charity Classic. You spell classic with a, 'K' and you've got COCK. I can see people all over Houston walking around with T-shirts that say COCK on them."

I was laughing pretty hard and so was Marty, and Milt finally looked at the two of us and hollered, "You're not helping!"

Monte asked, "Marty, what do you think of my idea?"

"I've got to be honest," Marty started to answer. "I like your idea. But call me old fashioned or just a heterosexual, but I can't wear a T-shirt that spells cock."

"You're looking at this the wrong way," Monte said. "Cock attracts women."

"It might also attract gays," I offered.

"I hadn't thought of that," said Monte. He then said through a laugh, "Back to the drawing board."

Alex, Steven, Fred, and Monte were all laughing as they headed out the door and Milt yelled to them, "Our tournament isn't going to be called COCK!"

As Milt yelled the word "cock," the waitress Patty entered the office with some paperwork for Milt. As she handed it to him she said, "I agree with you on that, Milty. I'm not saying I don't like cock but it isn't a good name for the tournament."

I smiled at Patty as she walked out of the room and Milt just glared at Marty and me. The dust had not settled from the comics' ideas for the name of the tournament when the very large and very black Marcella Mississippi came booming into the office. She went right after Milt and Marty as she yelled, "I know I can't pass the physical for your golf tournament, because I don't have any balls between my legs, they're in my golf bag where they belong!" I smiled because Milt and Marty looked liked two little boys who had just gotten caught doing something and were now going to get a lecture.

Marcella continued. "But I'm here to tell you that I can hit a golf ball better than most of the comics and so can some of the other comediennes and comedy club waitresses around this state. I just want you to know that if you're planning on having a 'Dicks Only' golf tournament, or if you're planning on having it at one of those country clubs that don't allow women or blacks, this whole thing will blow up in your faces. I'll kill two birds with one stone when my big black behind shows up there and it won't be to do any cooking or cleaning!"

Milt just put his head down on his desk as Marty murmured, "Oh, shit."

Marcella then looked over at me and winked as she said, "Hi, Dale."

Marcella was from New Orleans and she was everybody's favorite person and comic. When she was onstage all of the bar personnel and other comics would watch her. If an audience was a little stiff, she would tell them, "Don't slow down on me, white people! If you don't laugh I'll follow you home and hang out in your neighborhoods until the property value goes down!"

Marcella loved to make me blush, like the night she told me, "Dale, can you get some handcuffs from your dad? Because my biggest sexual fantasy has to do with a white boy and a pair of handcuffs."

I winked at Marcella and snuck out of Milt and Marty's office before she started in on them again. As I was going out the door, Milt was whining, "Marcella, honey . . ."

"Don't you "honey" me!"

Marty jumped in. "Marcella, we need you with us not against us. All of the comics will fall in line if you back us on this thing."

As I reentered the show room, even more comics and comedy club personnel had shown up. I saw someone I didn't expect to see: Dr. Dan Hollingsworth—or "The Professor" as everyone called him—was standing at the bar getting a lecture in comedy from a couple of the comics. The Professor's lectures at the University of Houston were always packed because they were so entertaining. His goal was to be the next Mort Sahl, the political humorist, which was why he used The Comedy Werks on Monday nights, to see if he could make it as a comedian. He always ended up his Monday evenings walking to his car and muttering "morons" under his breath.

One of comics was saying to him, "Comedy 101, Professor. If they don't get the premise they won't get the bit. You were talking down to them again last Monday night and that's why you bombed."

The Professor responded, "And then some idiot went onstage after me and got big laughs playing 'The Eyes of Texas' by doing arm farts."

"At least the audience understood what he was doing," added a second comic.

I asked The Professor why he was there that afternoon and he answered, "I'm here for the same reason I go to stock car races. I like high-speed collisions and I think that's what we are going to see here today."

I didn't get a chance to question The Professor about that because we were interrupted by comedian Barry Stein. "A comics golf tournament? And the whole idea is to raise enough money to pay for the damage the comics will do to the golf course."

Barry didn't wait for a response, he rarely did. He was a transplanted New Yorker whose act was as fast paced as the city he left behind. Barry was a prop comic and after he told us what he thought about the idea for The Comics Open, he continued walking along, picking up things off the bar, and giving them a caption to them like he did in his act. He picked up a large round saucer that a pizza had been served on and he yelled, "An IUD for an elephant!"

He picked up a black ashtray and held it to his cheek and said, "A beauty mark for a very large woman!"

Marcus Pauley started to hand Barry a bottle opener off the bar to see what he would make of it, and then Marcus turned the opener on Barry like it was a knife as Barry yelled, "A Jew being robbed by a black man!"

"Dale!" I heard my named called from behind me. I turned and at first I saw no one until I looked down and saw Billy Meyer, the smaller half of the comedy team of Bill and Billy.

Billy continued, "I want your dad to arrest my partner for impersonating a comedian! I want him charged with defrauding an audience and loitering onstage in front of a curtain! He should be charged with being an oversized load!"

I tried to say something but Billy went on with his tirade, "I'll be in the tournament but I won't play with my partner. Riding in the same cart with him is completely out of the question and I don't even want him in the same foursome as me. That gorilla-Godzilla-Big Foot-Lurch-Frankenstein-untalented-giant-scum-bag-whale-shit-smelling-Rodan-Brahma Bull-two quart-a-day-cum drinking bastard!"

Billy was as short as his partner was tall and as small as his partner was big. Bill Blevens was six foot five and weighed about two hundred and sixty pounds and Billy was five foot five and weighed about one forty. Neither one of them was very funny individually, but one night during an improv session they teamed up and the magic happened and a comedy team was born. They were very funny and they worked a lot but hated the fact they needed each other.

Big Bill Blevens added a new police code: "Five-O-Five, Attitude in Progress." Billy never understood that the code was about him. He was five foot five and whenever he was around there was definitely an "attitude in progress."

There was a comedy hall of fame story about Bill and Billy comics loved to tell. It took place at a comedy club in San Antonio. Bill and Billy had been bickering all week and they both had a few too many drinks Friday night between shows, and on their second show it all came out.

Bill told Billy, "You ain't any bigger than my cock."

Billy answered, "Well, keep your hands off me them, because I know how much you play with your cock."

Bill said, "My underwear is bigger than you."

Billy came back with, "I know, I know, everything about you is big. The only thing single digit about you is your IQ."

Bill must have really been drunk because he committed a cardinal error by asking Billy a question. Billy had an answer for absolutely any question. "Have you ever had sex with a normal-sized-woman?"

Billy answered, "No, but I did fuck your girlfriend, that Amazon bitch."

The audience went crazy, the comedy club owner went into shock, and the headliner on the show ran to the telephone to start calling other comics to tell them what was going on. The audience thought it was a big finale takeoff on television wrestling, because Bill had Billy held up over his head and they were both screaming as Billy was being scraped across the ceiling knocking down bits of plaster.

The review of that show was blown up, put into plastic, and placed beneath the picture of Bill and Billy on the wall of The Comedy Werks. A reviewer from a local San Antonio newspaper wrote in his column, "The comedy team of Bill and Billy can only be described as Laurel and Hardy on acid. They are, in fact, funny and they are definitely exciting, but in the same way an earthquake is exciting." The reviewer closed by saying, "Bill and Billy appear to get along only slightly better than the Arabs and Israelis."

There were as many questions as ideas about the tournament from the comics in the show room. The most often asked one was, "Do you have to know how to play golf to play in the tournament?"

Linda Hart wandered over. Linda was blond with big breasts. She was a singing impressionist who was very good, but she had no jokes for her act when she showed up at The Comedy Werks until she met Clay, who wrote her some funny lines and some song parodies. She thanked Clay that first night by getting drunk with him and rolling around in the back of his car with him.

She asked, "Does someone sing the national anthem before a golf tournament? Like they have a celebrity sing the national anthem before a football or baseball game? I would love to sing the national anthem before our golf tournament."

"I've never heard of that but it's our tournament and we can do whatever we want," I replied.

Rick Perry, the head bartender of The Laff Inn Comedy Club, yelled across the room to comedian Jimmy Clark, "Hey, Jimmy! You been to bed yet?"

Jimmy Clark was the comic who got his nose broken in the show room of The Comedy Werks the night Bobby Ray Sutton showed up and demonstrated how to swing a golf club. Jimmy's nasal passages opened the Friday before the meeting and he had been on a cocaine run and hadn't been to sleep since. Jimmy just gave Rick and everyone in the room a glazed-over look as he just smiled.

The stage was set with a blackboard as well as a table with three chairs. The meeting was called to order at noon by Milt as he rolled his wheelchair onto the stage. He was followed by his brother, Bobby Ray Sutton, and Brenda, who was carrying a cup of coffee. One of the comics yelled, "Hey, Brenda! Is that your coffee or are you back to waitressing?"

It got a small amount of laughter and Brenda didn't seem to mind but Milt snapped at the comic who said it, "We're not going to have any of that today. There's a lot we've got to get straight today and we don't have time for stuff like that."

The room fell quiet and everyone was kind of shocked because they had never seen Milt snap about something as trivial as that. Milt didn't know it then but he got the meeting off to the wrong kind of start. The bartender, comic Brent Harris, cut the tension a bit by asking, "Is the bar open?"

There was a nice laugh and Milt smiled and said, "Just for coffee—it's too early for anything else."

Jimmy Clark did a line from one of the comics' favorite old western movies and yelled, "Aw, come on! Beer ain't drinking!"

Marty had written the words "The Comics Open" across the top of the blackboard as everyone was talking. Milt finally noticed and pointed to it as he said adamantly, "The name of our tournament is The Comics Open. It's not anything else. That name tells exactly what it is, it's comics and open means golf tournament. Everyone will know what it means and what it is. There has been a lot of talk and suggestions about funny and silly names for the tournament, but we can only have one name for our tournament. Anything else or anything more would be confusing to the public, so it's The Comics Open and that's final."

Alex Day, who had already tried in Milt and Marty's office, tried again. "I still think putting the words, Everybody Duck—"

Milt immediately cut him off with, "No! None of that shit! You've all had fun coming up with a million names and you couldn't agree on one, even if I let you, so the name is there," as he pointed at the blackboard again. He added, "Again, that's final."

Everyone could feel the tension and no one could ever remember Milt acting like that or being in that kind of mood before. As usual, when Milt was in trouble his brother Marty came to the rescue. "Everybody, this tournament is absolutely a great idea for everyone involved, especially you comedians. It will promote all of the comedy clubs that want to get involved and all of the comics in Houston as well. We will get sponsors to put up money and gifts. The gifts will be for the comics and you comedy club personnel—things like golf shirts and sweaters—and the money will go to your favorite charities, which you will have to agree on."

Marty was doing what he did best: talking business and selling people on what he wanted to sell them. He had his audience's full attention as he continued, "Not everybody can actually play in the tournament, but that's not what this whole thing is about. There will be a banquet and a show in a building big enough to hold all of the people that would want to pay to see that. It will be the biggest comedy show in the history of the city or at least in the history of comedy clubs. Maybe we can have it videotaped and sold to a network or to cable, I don't know. But the least it will be is *big* with the most and the best Houston comedians—and comedians who have been invited from out of town, but who have performed at a Houston comedy club. It will be an incredible show."

Marty was interrupted by Harry Bosco who asked, "Which comedians? Who decides who qualifies to be on that show?"

Everyone in the room started to murmur. Harry had really hit on a key question. Marty quickly answered, "That is one of the many big questions we have to work out today. Before we tackle that one, I want to introduce your official board of directors of The Comics Open and that is the four people on this stage. Milt and me and local golf pro and legend, Bobby Ray Sutton."

Bobby Ray stood halfway up and waved a little to a smattering of applause and Marty continued, "And your very own comic-slash-golfer Brenda Brookshire."

Brenda smiled a little nervous smile. There was not much of an ovation, but she did receive twice the amount of applause that Bobby Ray got, and then someone in the back yelled in a serious tone, "Who elected you people?"

The room got quiet as the comics and comedy club personnel mulled over the question and then Larry Lawrence cut the tension by asking, "Why aren't there any gays on the board of directors?" That got a nice laugh from everyone in the room and Marty, who was not known for cracking jokes, put his hands on Bobby Ray's shoulders and said to Larry, "How do you know there's not any?"

After that laugh, Marty got serious. "Somebody had to take charge and get this thing going," he said. "Milt is the juggernaut behind this thing. He is the one who's making it happen. He decided who would be on the board. Milt's got a lot of connections with local television, radio, and the papers, so he will be great with promotion. Rumor has it that I'm a halfway decent businessman, so I will be taking care of that end and the details you people would never want to do. Bobby Ray Sutton is a natural because he's a member of the PGA Tour and a local boy. He will add a little credence to the tournament and he can help get us a country club to play at and help attract sponsors. And Brenda is a local gal who is a comic and golfer and—"

Before Marty could finish, another voice from the back of the room yelled out, "Hey, Brenda! Which one of them did you have to sleep with to get on that board?"

No one thought that was very funny—especially Brenda. Before she could verbalize a comeback, her old friend Bobby Sanchez came to her rescue and yelled at the comic who had said it, "Shut up, asshole!"

The comic just stared in Bobby's direction and it was fairly quiet and then Larry Lawrence stood up and yelled, "That's right! Shut up, asshole!"

There were a few giggles and then the comic yelled at Larry, "I'll take that from a Mexican but not from a faggot!" There was as much tension in the room as there was laughter. I just shook my head. I knew what the problem was. Comics are great at spreading fun and laughter but are terrible at creating and running the arena where they would spread that fun and laughter. It was the only time that many comedians had been in a show room and had really not known what to do. Comics don't know what to do at an organizational or business meeting. Show business is two words: "show" and "business." Almost all of the comedians I had known had been great at the one and horrible at the other. They were great at the show but had no talent for the business.

Marty tried to take control again as he said, "Okay, let's take Alex's question first, which was which comics qualify to play in the tournament and why. But before that, let's decide on which bartenders, waitresses, and managers. The only criteria I can think of is how long someone must have worked for a comedy club to qualify to be in the tournament."

Hank Bruno, the owner of The Comedy Corral, yelled out, "Two years."

Marty said, "Two years? That sounds fair. So it's two years."

"Wait a minute!" yelled Marcus Pauley who was standing at the back of the room not far from me. Marcus had always hated Hank Bruno because when Marcus first tried out at his club, Hank told him he didn't think his Angry Young Black Man act was funny and he didn't like his attitude in general. Marcus just figured Hank did not like blacks. Marcus continued, "Why does he have a say in that? He's not a bartender, a waitress, or a manager. Why does he have a say?"

"You're not either," shot back Hank Bruno.

Rick Perry, the bartender from The Laff Inn, jumped in the middle of the argument by saying, "It's not for either one of you to say. One of you is a comic and the other is a club owner, so it's not for either of you to have a say about the bar personnel."

Marty jumped back in, "Okay, Rick, what do you think? How long should someone have worked at a comedy club before they qualify to be involved in this tournament?"

Rick made everyone laugh when he said, "Two years." Hank Bruno smirked at Marcus who just glared in his direction.

"Milt, can we open the bar?" asked Jimmy as everyone laughed.

"No!" Milt shot back. "We've got work to do today. And by the way, we're going to do a shotgun start at this tournament, which means eighteen foursomes go to each tee and tee off all at once. So only seventy-two people can play. I figure we'll fill some of the spots with any television people who help us out and I know a couple of radio DJs who said they want to play. Bobby Ray mentioned that some of the sponsors he's rounding up will want to play and we'll have to let 'em. So, what I'm trying to say is not everyone of you is going to play."

"I thought this tournament was for us!" yelled a comedian who was standing in the back.

A waitress from The Comedy Corral yelled, "Oh, I get it! You just want us to work this thing! Well, I'm either playing or I'm going to get paid if I have to work it!"

Larry Lawrence cried, "I just want to be somebody's caddy!"

There was a lot of loud mumbling going on and Milt tried to shout over the noise. "But it's a charity! And it's good for all of us! Some of us will have to donate a lot of our time to make this thing work!"

"Sounds like 'our' time, not yours!" the waitress from The Comedy Corral yelled back and the mumbling started to get louder. Milt looked like he was getting mad and Bobby Ray and Brenda looked a little nervous.

Marty tried to take control again as he said, "So, two years! That's what you have decided on for involvement by any comedy club personnel! They have to have worked at a comedy club for at least two years!" Things calmed down a little bit so Marty stopped shouting. "Now, let's move on to Alex's question. The criteria for a comic playing in the tournament."

"No hacks!" came a voice out of the back of the room and all of the comedians started yelling their agreement, "Yeah! No hacks! Right on! Absolutely no hacks!"

"That calls for a round of drinks!" Jimmy tried to yell over the crowd.

Comedians who were dedicated to their craft hated the comedians who weren't and called them "hacks." A hack was a comedian who had no business being onstage and who had never had an original thought in his or her life. A hack didn't have an onstage persona and stole a little stage presence from a real comic, as well as some mannerisms from as many comedians as necessary. A hack also did the same when it came to creating comedy material. A hack, needless to say, did not have the respect of his or her peers.

Milt raised his hands as did Marty and everyone quieted as Milt said, "I'm way ahead of you" and produced a piece of paper. "I want you to decide but here is an outline. First of all, we can't have any newcomers, meaning open-mikers—people that are just starting out." No one said a word of protest, so Milt continued and went through most of his list. "Only working comics who have been at it at least two years and have been out on the circuit performing standup comedy. Any L.A., New York or other out-of-town comics could be invited only if they have performed at any of the Houston comedy clubs for at least a week a year."

Milt told them that he, along with the majority of the comics, would make a list as to which comedians would be invited to play and perform at the banquet. Marty was proud of the way Milt got through that part of the meeting without any problems. Milt's last comment was a one-word question to the comics. "Okay?"

"Okay!" they all yelled back. Then Jimmy Clark shouted, "That settles it then! Let's open the bar!"

The best part of the meeting was soon followed by the beginning of the worst as the subject turned to sponsors, and Bobby Ray decided he should talk for a while. That, and an old boyfriend of Brenda's decided to start pushing her buttons. Marty said, "Now, on the subject of sponsors," and without warning Bobby Ray interrupted him and stood up. While Bobby Ray was getting out of his chair, a comic by the name of Neil Holcome yelled from *his* chair, "Hey, Brenda! Just what is it you do on the board of directors?"

There were a few giggles and it was an embarrassing moment for Brenda. Brenda hated to be embarrassed by men, especially in public, and Neil knew that. Neil was emceeing the Monday night open mike show at Jokesters Comedy Club downtown, when he met Brenda. She snuck down there to go onstage before she ever went on at The Comedy Werks. It was a vulnerable time for her and Neil knew it and took full advantage of it. They dated twice, and as flattered as Brenda was, she knew in her gut that it wasn't right. She finally listened to her instincts and Neil didn't end up getting what he wanted. He had been nasty to her ever since and he was pretty good at pushing her buttons and making her crazy when he wanted to.

Marty was concerned because he didn't know what Bobby Ray was going to say and was worried that he might upset the comedians. "I'm personally taking this tournament into the big time," Bobby Ray said through a wide smile. "You don't have to thank me now, but I'm working on some of the same people who sponsor some of the PGA events I play in."

Marty knew comedians didn't like people who seemed to be impressed with themselves and Bobby Ray was coming off as very impressed with himself. Milt noticed something worse: Bobby Ray was getting very comfortable on the stage. Milt's worst fears were realized when Bobby Ray tried to tell a joke. "I'm known as a pretty funny guy out on the PGA Tour. I'm always telling funny stories. Like one tournament I was in, the two best balls I hit were—"

"When you stepped on a rake!" as almost everyone there yelled out the punch line. Milt and Marty shook their heads. They wondered just how stupid Bobby Ray must be to think he could run one of the oldest jokes in the world past a room full of comedians and comedy club personnel.

Bobby Ray was seething.

Big Bill Blevens stood up and said to Bobby Ray, "I was thinking, sure you can get some big sponsors and so can Milt and Marty, but this is also a city that most of us have lived in our whole lives. We know a lot of small businesses that would love to be part of something like this. They couldn't donate a lot of money but they could donate services like free hair cuts, car tuneups, movie tickets, and stuff like that. A lot of our friends and relatives are involved in small businesses like that."

Bobby Ray, who was still smarting from everyone yelling out the punch line to his joke, shot back to Big Bill, "I said I was taking this tournament into the big time. I'm talking Titleist, McGregor, Spalding, and even a major supermarket chain. Possibly a car company. Nobody cares if your aunt can cut somebody's hair while your uncle changes the oil in their car."

The room went silent and Brenda said under her breath, "Oh, God."

Bill's partner Billy stood up and said to Bobby Ray, "Asshole. You just stepped on that rake again."

All Bobby Ray had accomplished was to turn the comedians and all of the comedy club personnel against him. Marty just about threw Bobby Ray back into his chair as he yelled over the rumblings in the room, "Okay! Bobby Ray might have made a little mistake there, but he has been working hard on getting the sponsors for the tournament! He didn't word it the right way but he's on our side!"

A comic yelled out of the crowd, "I'm not so sure whose side he is on! My parents have a little restaurant and they were interested in getting involved in this! My folks are on our side, but I'm not so sure the retarded son of Arnold Palmer there is!"

Marty thought his brother had lost his mind when Milt said, "It just so happens Bobby Ray isn't wrong about that. We are trying to keep the sponsorship big and big companies don't want to be on the same page in the program as a mom-and-pop pizza joint or a place you get your oil changed. The board of directors is going to be in charge of who qualifies to be a sponsor of this tournament or not."

None of us in the room could believe Milt had just said that. Things went from bad to worse when Hank Bruno, the only other comedy club owner there, said, "They are both right. We're trying to do this thing right. We ain't trying to get sponsors for a bowling league like where they wear crappy fake satin jackets with Harry's Bail Bonds printed on the back."

Marcus Pauley yelled from the back of the room, "You don't know shit, Bruno!"

"I know you ain't funny!" Bruno yelled back.

Things were getting bad. I got up off my barstool.

Barry Stein, the prop comic, yelled, "So the board that no one elected is going to decide everything from which comics to which sponsors?"

Marty tried to say something but was cut off by Tony Gato, a comic friend of Barry's from New York, who was in town performing at The Laff Inn. "The comics in New York tried to organize a benefit for street people last year," he said. "And everything was running smoothly until the comedy club owners decided they had to take it over. It always goes like that. The people that do all of the work come up with something good and management feels they have to take it over."

The mood of the room really turned ugly when Tony used the word "management." There really hadn't been any battle lines drawn until then; it had been just a series of disagreements and arguments. But when Tony said "management," sides were taken and the fight was on.

"What the hell do you mean?" Milt cried in disbelief. "This isn't a goddamned labor-management meeting!"

"Maybe it should be!" someone shouted from the crowd.

Jimmy Clark yelled, "Yeah! Why can't we get booze when we want it?"

The straw that broke the camel's back was Neil Holcome's question to Brenda, "Hey, Brenda! When did you get into bed with management?"

Brenda, who had not said one word during the entire meeting, screamed, "Fuck you, Neil Holcome! You little cock sucker!"

Larry Lawrence, suddenly interested, asked, "Who's a cock sucker?" as Brenda jumped from the stage and tried to go after Neil Holcome. Two people got in front of Brenda as Marty jumped off the stage and grabbed her from behind. Soon everyone in the room was screaming, and Marcus Pauley started to go for Hank Bruno, who was moving his girlfriend out of the way.

Neil Holcome yelled, "Hey, Brenda! When did you lose your sense of humor?"

Brenda screamed, "The only thing smaller than your sense of humor is your dick!"

Billy Meyer hollered up to Bobby Ray as he made his way toward the stage, "Hey, you PGA fuck! You ought to get a hospital to sponsor you because you're going to need one when I get through with you!"

Bobby Ray yelled back at Billy, "Well, come on then! You ain't any bigger than a golf ball and I've knocked the shit out of enough golf balls in my life, so get your tiny ass up here!"

Big Bill grabbed Billy from behind and picked him up and yelled up to Bobby Ray, "Let me even this thing up a little bit sizewise."

Brent Harris and I were holding back Marcus Pauley, and a bartender from The Comedy Corral held onto Hank Bruno. Bobby Ray stayed up on the stage because he didn't like the size of Big Bill. Billy kept yelling things like, "What's PGA stand for? Pretty gutless asshole?" Brenda kept screaming and trying to swing at Neil Holcome as Milt bellowed from the stage, "This is fucking ridiculous!"

Larry Lawrence jumped up onto the stage and with his right hand over his heart started to sing "God Bless America" as Jimmy Clark yelled from the bar, "Okay! Let's all have a drink and settle down!"

One of the comics yelled, "We'll have our own tournament!"

"Good!" Milt yelled back to him. "Have your own fucking tournament, because I'm not going to be involved in this one!"

Comedy club people weren't usually prone to violence but I had to admit I had never seen them so angry. Tempers were hot and Harry Bosco asked me, "Which side are you on, Dale?"

I'm glad I got a laugh from the few guys who knew The Comics Open was my idea when I said, "Right now I feel like Abraham Lincoln. Freeing the slaves seemed like such a great idea but who knew it was going to start a civil war?"

Milt quit the tournament and board of directors. So did Bobby Ray. All of the comedians pulled out of the tournament, as well as all of the comedy club personnel. They all pouted pretty hard for a few days, but by Wednesday, the tournament was back on again.

It had been a tough job, but I was responsible for bringing all of the comedians and comedy club personnel back together for the tournament. I decided to win them back one at a time if I had to, and that's basically how it started. I would talk to them one on one and in groups of three, four, or more. I kept telling the comics, "Imagine this whole golf tournament thing as being just like The Comedy Werks. Milt and Marty are running it, they're going to do the best they can and they're going to be fair just the way they've always been. Just like The Comedy Werks, they're not going to be able to make everybody happy. Everybody thinks they should be getting more stage time and more gigs, but Milt and Marty do the best they can, and they are always fair."

The comics hated Bobby Ray Sutton. I handled that issue by telling them, "You don't have to like the PGA golfer. All he's doing is getting sponsors that are going to give y'all nice prizes, gifts and money for your favorite charities." Everyone I spoke to responded positively and the word spread to all of the comedy clubs in less than forty-eight hours.

Marty never did quit the tournament and Brenda wasn't about to because of that comment by Neil Holcome. Marty had a bit of a tough time getting Bobby Ray back, but he explained how important he was to the tournament. He also explained how good Bobby Ray was going to look on television at the press conference. Marty lied a bit as he said, "That's what I was saving you for, Bobby Ray. I didn't want you to talk at that organizational meeting because I wanted you to save all of your talking for the press conference."

The press conference was held two weeks later in the show room of The Comedy Werks, just like the organizational meeting had been, but the press conference was to be nothing at all like the fiasco the organizational meeting had been. The press conference was where the real trouble started.

CHAPTER FIVE

A lot had happened in the two weeks between the organizational meeting and the press conference. Bobby Ray quit trying to line up the posh, super-private, super-elite country clubs and decided to go with the one he grew up and learned on. It was semiprivate because it had members, but it was an open-to-the-public course in the neighborhood he grew up in El Rancho Heights. The El Rancho Heights Golf Course would be perfect for the tournament. It had a lot of parking room for all the people who would be coming to see the event.

The members of The El Rancho Heights Golf Course would do anything their favorite son asked and jumped at Bobby Ray's idea. They loved the idea of a tournament for charity. The publicity could only help their course. I happened to ride out with Bobby Ray, Milt, and Marty to check the place out and all the members seemed to genuflect when Bobby Ray walked in.

Three old-timers walked up to us and one of them pointed at Bobby Ray, saying, "I watched that boy grow up on this course."

Another one added, "I watched him play here as a kid and then on television in the PGA."

I wanted to add, "My dad told me that Bobby Ray was arrested for indecent exposure one night," but I didn't think it was the right time and place to share that information.

Bobby Ray took the banner out of the clubhouse that had the words "El Rancho Heights Golf Course" on it, and he told the members he was going to display it at the press conference.

Marty had been running into unexpected problems trying to get a theater for the show after the tournament. He was surprised the theater owners and managers didn't jump at his idea. Sure, they liked the idea of a charity show, but they weren't that fond of comedy clubs and especially low-level comedians. They kept mentioning their operating costs, and then there was the matter of insurance and security for a show like that.

Marty finally followed Bobby Ray's lead, which was to go back to his roots. He returned to the place where he and Bobby Ray met—El Rancho Heights High School. Milt and Marty felt that it was the perfect place for their show after Bobby Ray secured The El Rancho Heights Golf Course. The high school was only two blocks from the golf course. So both events would be close together.

The high school didn't jump at the idea either but finally went along with their three somewhat famous alumni. Milt and Marty assured their alma mater that some of the charity funds would be diverted to the drama department and to help buy equipment for the marching band. Milt couldn't wait to be the first comic to perform in his old high school auditorium that seated twelve hundred people.

So the sites for both events were set and so was the date. It was all to happen on the third Monday in June, which was the Monday after the beginning of high school summer vacation. The press conference for the event was to be held in the show room of The Comedy Werks exactly one month before the tournament and show.

I had to make a special trip downtown to Jokesters Comedy Club to talk to Neil Holcome. My opening statement to him was, "What's between you and Brenda is your business, but she doesn't need any aggravation while this tournament is going on. She's real proud to be on the board of directors, she's going to play in the tournament and perform in the show, and there could be a problem if you're around. Neil, what I'm trying to tell you is that, you're not welcome at the tournament or the show afterwards."

There was a long pause and then Neil thanked me for coming down to talk to him personally. He added, "Dale, I just don't appreciate being told where I can't go and what I can't do. I'm a comedian and I have just as much right to go to the tournament and take part in that show as anybody else."

At that point I played what I figured was the first of my two trump cards. "You're right, Neil," I said. I couldn't agree with you more, but I'm just trying to stop the problem before it starts. And I'm not going to threaten you because I'm not going to have anything to do with it. But Bobby Sanchez is Brenda's best friend and if you upset her again like you did at that meeting, he says he's going to go one-on-one with you in an ass-kicking contest."

I could tell by Neil's expression that he was caving in. I gave him a nice way out when I played my second trump card. "Neil, I was thinking that with all the comics coming to town, it would be a good time to pick some of the best jobs out of town. You could have your pick of just about any job you wanted at just about any comedy club outside of Houston the week before the tournament and the week of the tournament. I talked to Milt and Marty about it and they not only agree, they're willing to set it up."

I closed with that offer and Neil did the smart thing and went along with it. He was more than happy to pick up a couple of weeks of out-of-town work. He decided to pass on the tournament and the show and the probable ass-kicking by Bobby Sanchez.

The first real signs of excitement started to show in the comedy community as the day of the press conference arrived. I noticed that the comics were starting to act like animals. It reminded me of a nature show I once saw on TV. The comics were trying to act discreet but they were running in packs more and sniffing the air. They didn't know exactly what was going on but they knew things were starting to get exciting. They knew they might have a chance to take down something really big.

The press conference was held on the third Monday in May, at noon, in the show room of The Comedy Werks. Milt wanted it to be big and entertaining, and it ended up surpassing his wildest expectations. Milt was always good with the press and he told the newspaper reporters, the disc jockeys, and the television people, "Not just because it's for charity and not just because it's good for Houston, but for your own sake, do not miss this press conference."

The press took Milt's advice and they showed up in droves. Every Houston newspaper, large and small, was represented as well as the three main television stations, two of the small ones, and six of the radio stations. By noon the parking lot and parking spaces in front of The Comedy Werks were filled with news trucks and vans. Just about every news vehicle in Houston was there except for the three news helicopters and they finally showed up because the police helicopter did.

Milt and Marty never organized anything as well as they organized the press conference. I think they put in more time planning that press conference than they ever did planning the opening of their club.

I sat in on a couple of the meetings in their office and the message was always the same. Milt would say, "The press conference is the thing, not the tournament and the show." Marty would add, "The tournament and show don't even matter unless the press conference is a giant success."

The press conference was scheduled to start in the show room at noon but that was just a ploy to get everyone there. Few people knew it, but the show was to start at eleven forty-five in front of The Comedy Werks. And the show would start on the street—not in the club.

Since it was a Monday, the King of Monday Nights was in town and he would be going onstage later that night. Jake Davis billed himself as "The Trucker Comic." He was also known as "King of Monday Nights" because by that time he had performed on an open-mike night at a comedy club in almost every state in the continental United States. Alaska didn't have a comedy club and he couldn't get to Hawaii by truck.

He was five feet nine inches tall and the only thing bigger than his chest was his stomach and his butt. He had a short beard and always wore a cowboy hat, boots, Levi's and a belt with a big buckle. He wore a red scarf he used to wipe sweat off his face, and he always had a beer with him onstage.

The first time I met Jake was on a Monday night at The Comedy Werks. Jake followed Marcus Pauley, who had hit the audience hard with his angry young black man act. Jake's opening statement was, "I agree with the man that was just up here. I hate white people too. I never really thought about it until I listened to him, but white people have been the cause of all of my problems, too. Starting with my parents, who happened to be a white couple, they were pretty rough on me. My first two wives were white and there's two reasons to hate white people right there."

He also said from the stage that night, "I hate the way that most people think that truckers are high on speed, eating amphetamines, and snorting cocaine as we drive the highways of this country. That's not necessarily true, but come to think of it, I haven't been to sleep since last fall."

One night I introduced my dad to Jake at The Comedy Werks. After a fairly long conversation, Jake said to my dad, "This is the longest I've ever talked to an officer of the law who wasn't arresting me."

Promptly at eleven forty-five the morning of the press conference, Jake Davis rumbled down the street in front of The Comedy Werks in his big rig, blasting his horn and screaming into his microphone and out through the speaker in the grill of his truck, "I don't want to live and I don't care who I take with me!"

I had talked my dad into having a police car in close pursuit of Jake in his truck with the sirens blaring and red lights flashing as the cop kept yelling into his microphone, "Pull over!"

I also had it worked out with my dad that the police helicopter would show up. I knew that where the police helicopter went, so did the three news helicopters.

With the squad car in close pursuit, Jake went down about three blocks, then turned around to lead the squad car back toward The Comedy Werks. By that time everyone was outside to see the spectacle. Jake finally locked up his brakes and his truck and trailer just about jackknifed in front of The Comedy Werks.

Jake got out and started waving to the crowd as all the comedians and comedy club personnel cheered their approval. That's when the news people realized it was a stunt and they applauded too. The cop got out of the squad car and waved to the crowd and then shook hands with Jake. He then waved to the police helicopter and everyone waved to the news helicopters. It looked great on television and was the lead-in to the five o'clock news: "Why are all those people waving?" There was a big banner on each side of Jake's truck and the news people got pictures and videotape of them. The banners read, "THE COMICS OPEN HOUSTON." Under that in smaller print was "El Rancho Heights Golf Course" and under that "June 17." There were also logos in the corners of the banner of the four biggest sponsors.

There was food for everyone. Milt and Marty made the other club owners pay for the catering while they took care of the open bar. Waitresses Patty and Carolyn helped serve the press. They wore T-shirts with "The Comics Open" printed across the front with "Sponsored By The Comedy Werks" on the back. Waitresses and bartenders from other comedy clubs wore the same T-shirts except with the names of their comedy clubs on the back.

Jimmy Clark got himself a nice spot by the bar and was not shut out as he had been at the organizational meeting. Rick Perry of The Laff Inn was bartending along with Brent Harris and they both knew that they weren't to over-pour Jimmy. Jimmy was still hitting the cocaine and the booze pretty hard, and it was rumored he had only been to bed four times in the two weeks since the organizational meeting.

The show room had been completely decorated with green and white streamers and posters of golfers. There was a movie poster of Bing Crosby and Bob Hope wearing golf outfits and holding golf clubs. There was also a big picture poster of Bobby Ray Sutton with his name across the bottom and the words "Houston's Finest."

Behind the stage was another big banner like the ones that were on the sides of Jake's truck. The banner Bobby Ray had taken from The El Rancho Heights Golf Course was also displayed prominently. There were four smaller banners on the wall with more of the sponsors' logos, including one for an athletic clothing company, one for the biggest supermarket chain in Houston, an oil company had one and a sporting goods store.

Milt insisted on a podium so they could best display The Comedy Werks name. Also on the podium, but in not as large letters, were the names of the rest of the comedy clubs in town. The Laff Inn was on there, as well as The Comedy Corral, Jokesters, The Laff A Lot, and Hilarities.

The podium was in the middle of the stage and just to stage left was an opening for Milt's wheelchair. To the left of that was a table with five chairs and a microphone to be passed to whoever was to speak or answer questions from the press. There were five TV news cameras around the back of the show room. Everything was ready, and the press conference started at just a few minutes after noon.

It began just like a show with the lights going down and some taped music coming up. One of the comics made an offstage announcement into the sound system welcoming everyone to the press conference for "The Comics Open." The press people were very surprised, especially when they were asked to "please welcome to the stage Houston comedian Harry Bosco!"

Harry took the stage and welcomed everyone and explained that, besides doing standup comedy, he also did a lot of improvisational comedy at The Comedy Werks and the other comedy clubs around Houston. "We were kind of wondering," he said, "what was going to happen at the press conference for The Comics Open and what the questions would be like." With that, a series of comedians approached Harry, some wearing hats that said "Press" on them and all carrying either note pads or small tape recorders.

The first question for Harry came from Big Bill Blevens who said, "I'm Pervis Medville of the *Houston Rag and Shopper*. About this Comics Open—are you a comic or a golfer?"

Harry answered, "Both."

"Which are you better at? Golf or comedy?"

"I'm a funny golfer," replied Harry.

"What are your goals for the tournament?"

"To raise a lot of money for charities, to play well in the tournament, to have a good set at the show afterwards, and then get drunk and have sex with somebody's girlfriend."

That was the first big laugh of the press conference and when it died down Greg Okada said to Harry, "I'm Stirfry Tempura of *The Galveston Gossip*. Is the owner of The Comedy Corral going to be involved in this tournament, especially now that those morals charges are hanging over his head?"

Harry snapped, "I want to say categorically that what a man does in the privacy of his own home with a sheep is no one else's business. I don't see what everybody got so upset about. All he did was dress the sheep up a little bit and the vet did verify that it was in fact a female sheep." The press especially liked that one and roared their approval.

Bobby Sanchez said, "I'm Frederico Manta Lunes Martes Miércoles of *The San Antonio Rumor*. The host comedy club of this tournament, The Comedy Werks, is co-owned by Milt Langely, who is being sued by two sets of parents of two underage girls. Any comment?"

"Those girls wanted a ride in Milt's wheelchair and as always he obliged!" Harry protested. "And I agree with what Milt said about the incident, 'Two girls at fifteen each add up to over eighteen.'"

The press loved the sketch and the fact that all of the questions had to do with the comedy club owners being degenerates and the comics wanting to get laid. Brent Harris puffed out his chest and said sternly, "I'm Abdul Akeem Mecca Washington of the *Houston Black Attitude.* Are black people going to be allowed to play in this tournament?"

Harry looked at the size of Brent. He looked at the audience, then back at Brent. "Yes, sir, and I will be your caddy."

The assembled people of the press laughed and applauded as Brent and Harry walked off the stage together. The lights came up and the theme from Ike and Tina Turner's "Proud Mary," started to play over the sound system. Marty pushed Milt to the stage, followed by Bobby Ray, Brenda, and Carl Stevens, who owned a sporting goods store and was one of the sponsors. There was also Bob Wurley, a representative from a sportswear company, and a woman by the name of Mrs. Helen Scoggins, who represented Children's Charities of Houston.

Marty welcomed everyone and thanked them for being there. He did a nice opening statement, introduced everyone onstage, and announced that more comics, comedy club owners, and comedy club personnel could take the stage whenever they felt like it. Marty then laid out the goals of the tournament and, unexpected to everyone there, he introduced me.

I walked up to the podium to a nice round of applause and the chants of the comics, "Dale! Dale!" When I got to podium I took out a piece of paper and said into the microphone, "I have here a short statement from the chief of police of Houston, Bertram Chase: 'We here at the department salute the comedy community of Houston for what you are doing and pledge our support to The Comics Open, although our support does not include get-out-of-jail-free cards for the comedians. Have fun and play fair.'"

I said, "Thank you," and received a nice round of applause as I walked over and took a seat onstage at the end the farthest away from the podium. Milt and Marty wanted me up on the stage because they had plans for me later in the press conference. They pointed to the chair that had my prop trench coat hanging over the back of it.

The press conference was then thrown open for questions and Milt answered the first series about how the tournament and show mix was a natural—good for everybody involved. How it would raise money for charities and draw attention to the comedians and comedy clubs of Houston. And how the tournament itself would be funny, but the show afterwards would be one of a kind with maybe twenty comics going onstage for ten minutes each.

Bobby Ray handled the questions about how he got involved—having known Milt and Marty in high school and having remained such good friends with them. He loved the idea of the tournament and being able to involve his old golf course, some sponsors, and people he knew through the PGA Tour. He got a little choked up when he said he loved Houston and was happy to have a chance to give something back to the community. He hurriedly passed the microphone to Brenda, as he bowed his head and wiped his eyes.

Bobby Ray seemed to start a trend of getting choked up. Many people who spoke after that seemed to get misty-eyed. Brenda started off funny talking about her fellow comic, Bobby Sanchez, and how they used to work in a restaurant and he would take her to a driving range and teach her how to grip and swing a club and hit a golf ball. She said, "We mostly just went to driving ranges because there weren't a lot of country clubs that were going to let a woman and a Mexican on their courses." The people of the press reacted with smiles and laughter.

Brenda gave a short but touching testimonial about what the comedy community of Houston and Houston itself meant to her. She tried to explain how honored she was to be selected to be on the board of directors of the golf tournament, but she got too choked up and handed the microphone to Bob Wurley, the representative from the sportswear company.

Bob Wurley was one of the few who didn't get emotional. His basic message was, "We're doing some exciting things with acrylics and we're glad to be a part of this tournament."

Milt smelled a whiff of marijuana smoke the same instant I did. We both glared in the direction of the back bar and dressing room. Brent and Rick Perry went into action as Brent turned on a blender to drown out the sound of the spray of air freshener, as Rick held the can in front of an air conditioning duct, and then sprayed it as he walked toward the dressing room. When he got to the dressing room door, a comic came out, coughing. He then looked to the stage where Milt was glaring at him and I gave him the knife across the throat sign.

As Bob Wurley was making his statement about acrylics, Hank Bruno was making his way to the stage. He had been moved by the emotion Bobby Ray and Brenda had shared with the audience, and he felt compelled to make a statement. He took the podium and said, "I'm Hank Bruno, owner of The Comedy Corral. I, too, am proud to be a Houstonian. I was born here, went to school here, and almost graduated from high school here, and I did some time here, but that's not important. I always wanted to belong to something good and important. I first had titty bars because I like women and then I saw the success these guys and The Laff Inn were having with comedy clubs, so I opened my own, even though I hate comics more than the bitches I used to have to work with."

The press people kept looking back and forth at one another as Hank kept talking, "I know the comics don't like me, but I want that to change. We have a tremendous chance to do some real good here and I want The Comedy Corral to lead the way! We're going to raise more money than any of the other comedy clubs! We're going to set the standard by which other comedy clubs will be judged in terms of raising money for these charities!"

A small roar started in the show room, led by Hank's girlfriend and his employees, as Milt and Marty stared at each other in disbelief. Milt whispered, "He doesn't understand. What the hell is he talking about?"

There was a quiver in Hank's voice and his eyes started to get moist as he said emphatically, "I know I've been a prick! But a man can change! I want this thing to be the most successful fund-raiser in the city's history and I pledge that The Comedy Corral will lead the way!"

Tears were streaming down Hank's face as he walked from the stage and started to make his way through the crowd, which was cheering and applauding. Marcus Pauley, who had always hated Hank Bruno, stuck out his hand to him and Hank stopped and gave Marcus his hand. They then hugged. Jimmy Clark, who was sitting at the back bar and had been on an alcohol and cocaine induced crying jag ever since Bobby Ray and Brenda spoke, blubbered. "That's the most beautiful thing I've ever seen! They hated each other! Now look at 'em! A white man and a black man!"

Milt glared at Brent and gave him the cut-off sign as he looked at Jimmy. Milt then said to his brother, "What the hell is going on here?"

Milt and Marty were glad to see a comic working his way to the stage and podium. "We need a little levity," Milt said to his brother.

It dawned on me what was happening. Comedians are a very competitive lot. If one of them was getting a laugh then each of them wanted to top that person, and then each other, with a funny one-liner or routine. The problem at the press conference was that the comics got into a competition of who could make the most outrageous pledge and emotional statement. It became evident that, as good as the comics were at being funny, that's how bad they were at being dramatic.

"You're not a Houston comic!" one of the comedians jokingly yelled from the back of the room as Steven Reed got to the podium. "He's right and he's wrong," was Steven's opening line. "He's confused, just like he is about his sexuality."

"That's more like it," Milt whispered to his brother as everyone was laughing.

"I'm Steven Reed and I am a Houston comic. I wasn't born here, but I started my career right here learning how to do it at The Comedy Werks. Now I am just about the full-time house emcee at The Laff Trap in Austin. All of the bar personnel there are excited about the tournament and the charities. Hank Bruno, you're right. You've been a prick! But we accept your challenge! Right now we are raising money in Austin for the charities in Houston! What do you think about that? Not even Hank Bruno or any other comedy club can make that statement!"

Everyone in the audience and onstage was cheering and applauding wildly and if anyone was listening closely, they could hear Jimmy Clark yelling at Brent Harris, "What do you mean I've had enough!"

When the cheering and applauding died down, Steven looked at Helen Scoggins and said seriously, "If a kid can laugh one more time because of us, if one child's last few days on this earth can be a little easier and happier because of our work, then all I can say is, 'I'm proud to be a Houston comic.'"

Everyone was cheering wildly again as Steven Reed walked from the stage wiping the tears from his eyes.

Milt whispered harshly to his brother, "Pathos and bullshit, that's all that's going on here. Get somebody funny up here now."

Marty quickly gestured to Clay to come to the stage and he immediately began making his way through the crowd as Helen Scoggins unexpectedly took the podium. There were tears in her eyes as she talked about the genuine commitment to the charities she had felt from the comedy community that day. She said, "I've never been around comedians or comedy club owners before but let me tell y'all something, I'm impressed." She closed her short statement by saying, "God bless Houston comedy!"

Clay took the podium as Helen rushed back to her seat onstage next to Bob Wurley. As she was wiping away her tears, Bob patted her on the back and told her what a fine job she had done. He also complimented her on the suit she was wearing and he asked her what fabric it was.

Clay's opening statement was, "I'm Deveraux Clay Clayton." He then started to spell his name so the newspaper people could get it right and everyone laughed at the joke. Clay continued, "I'm confused, but not about my sexuality." There was more laughter in the show room and Milt whispered to his brother, "That's more like it."

Clay caught everyone off guard when he said, "I thought the money for the charities would go to the comedians. By that, I mean there should be a fund for the comics at all the free clinics, because every comedian I know had the clap at least once. And I think some money should go to that home for unwed mothers, because the comedians of Houston and those passing through did the most to keep that home busy."

Everyone in the show room was laughing hysterically and the press—and Milt and Marty—were loving it. Clay continued, "And there should be a fund for the comedians alcohol and drug abuse program."

At that moment Jimmy Clark screamed at Brent Harris, "I said I want a fucking drink!"

Clay quickly said, "See, there's one now."

After seeing how much laughter Clay got, the other comedians decided to get back into the competition of trying to top each other. After Clay, Barry Stein the prop comic, went onstage with a golf bag full of things and did three minutes of rapid fire comedy. He pulled out a three wood that he had painted completely green and yelled, "The Jolly Green Giant's swizzle stick!" He pulled out a left-handed white sequined glove and yelled, "Michael Jackson's golf glove!" For his last joke he held up a rolled-up green sleeping bag as he said, "The Jolly Green Giant's condom!"

Milt and Marty liked the press corps' reaction to Barry jokes. They must have wanted to keep the comedy going because they looked over at me and nodded, meaning I would be next.

Barry was still getting a big round of applause as I stood up and put on my trench coat and walked to the podium in my impression of Peter Falk as Colombo. I was holding an unlit cigar in my right fingers and the audience quieted for my opening line, "Pardon me, am I bothering
you?" The audience laughed and they especially seemed to like the way I could contort my face to look just like Peter Falk.

As Colombo I told the audience I was looking for a murder suspect who ran from Los Angeles and was believed to be hiding in Houston. "The murder suspect is believed to be masquerading as either a comedian or a member of the Houston press corps, because no one is looking for Houston comedians or members of the Houston press corps."

I was feeling really confident so I decided to take a chance and take some questions from the press corps. I asked, "Are there any questions?"

I knew I couldn't miss answering as Colombo, rambling on, talking gibberish, and then saying, "I hope I made that perfectly clear."

I closed my time as Colombo by playing on a joke that was done earlier in the press conference. "I am currently involved with another murder investigation." I pointed as I said, "Hank Bruno of The Comedy Corral. That sheep you were involved with was found murdered and you are my number one suspect."

I then waved to the crowd and I got a great ovation as I slapped hands with everyone onstage while I walked back to my seat.

Everything was going great, but the trouble started with the comic who followed me onstage. Mark Silverman was an L.A. comic who worked for the entire Laff Inn chain. He was strictly an opening act and the only thing he was good at was emceeing. He didn't have any talent but loved the business and loved to talk. Mark had a bad habit of dropping celebrities' names as he tried to impress people by making them think he knew "Farrah," "Flip," "Robin," and "Chevy."

Mark took the podium and spoke seriously. "I couldn't be any more impressed with what's going on down here. I heard in L.A. that you were doing a charity comedians' golf tournament, but I had no idea it was this big and had the potential to do so much good. The guy that was just up here doing Peter Falk. I don't know Peter Falk but I do know Jerry Lewis and if I told him about this tournament and what it's doing, he would fly down."

The entire press corps perked up as did Milt, Marty, and myself. I immediately recognized the potential for trouble. Mark continued, "And Buddy is another one that loves golf. If he isn't in Vegas, Tahoe, or Atlantic City, I bet I could get him to come here."

A number of the press people raised their hands and Mark was absolutely loving the attention. One reporter asked, "Are you talking Jerry Lewis and Buddy Hackett?"

"Yes," answered Mark and the entire room was buzzing as reporters wrote on their note pads. Mark went on, "I could especially talk to some of the comics of this generation that have made it big and could help this tournament. I'm talking Gabe, J. J., and Billy just to name a few."

"Do you mean Gabe Kaplan, Jimmie Walker, and Billy Crystal?" a reporter asked.

"Yes," answered Mark and the room buzzed even more. David Hamilton, who was working with Mark that week and knew him from L.A., knew Mark loved to drop names. David told me later, "Sure, he has met those guys, but it was like they passed each other in a airport or restaurant. He really doesn't know them."

Mark Silverman's closing was even more disastrous than anything he had said up until then. "I know a lot of stars in comedy, TV, and film that would be interested in this once I tell them how organized it is and how the press is behind it. Many of these stars I have been talking about are, like me, Jewish. I think it would help, and I think right now we should just go ahead and pledge that Jewish charities in Houston should benefit from this tournament. Thank you very much."

No one could hear Milt scream, "He can't do that!" because almost everyone in the show room was cheering and applauding. Helen Scoggins ran over to shake Mark's hand and Milt was pulling on Marty's arm as he loudly whispered, "He can't pick which charity he wants money to go to. After the news tonight, Jewish temples and synagogues will be flooding our phone lines. He gets to be a big shot for a moment. He makes a bullshit statement like that and leaves town and I'll guarantee you he won't be back for the tournament because he won't be able to get any of those celebrities. And now each of the comics will want to pick their own charity."

Milt had hit the nail on the head because after that there was a parade of comedians to the podium who swore they could help raise money and then pledged where they thought it should go. Many of the comics also got caught up in the frenzy of dropping names and suggesting which celebrity they could get to show up. Names from the world of sports like Nolan Ryan, Earl Campbell, and Hakeem Olajuwon were filling the air as the press corps scribbled madly. One comic said, "They ain't Houston, but it couldn't hurt if I got some of the Cowboys to show up. I know my old buddy Roger Staubach would do it for me."

Marty was desperately trying to get everybody under control but Milt just pulled him into the chair next to him and said, "Let them go absolutely crazy. I really don't care at this point." Milt looked at me and then motioned to the bar and laughed as he said, "The only person who can control anybody is Big Bill." I looked at the back bar to see Bill Blevens holding Jimmy Clark in a headlock that looked more like a sleeper hold, because Jimmy wasn't moving. Milt looked back at all of the mayhem and said to me, "When the comics get done with this, it will be a celebrity tournament, and we'll owe over two hundred charities."

The show room and stage were still an orgy of celebrity name dropping and impossible promises from the comics as the press kept scribbling and the video cameras kept rolling. The whole room went silent and seemed to genuflect when Jake Davis mentioned Willie Nelson. He went on to say, "Now, I've never really met the man, but I mean I feel like I have. I had real good seats at a couple of his concerts. But I know that when I get the information to him he will show up and play in the tournament and perform in the show!"

Everyone was applauding wildly as Milt and I shook our heads and Marty tried to hide his. Jake continued, "For those of you who don't know me, I'm Jake Davis, The Trucker Comic, and I do comedy as well as drive a truck full-time. Lots of truckers do a lot of good work and do charities and all. There's the 'Truckers for Jesus,' 'Truckers for a Return to Segregation,' and the 'Truckers for Concealed Handguns.' Well, I just want to tell y'all something: when I drive from Louisiana through Beaumont on the outskirts of Houston, I always drive by a special school. I don't know the name of it but the kids look retarded; they're in the playground wearing football helmets and volunteers are wiping drool from their faces. It just breaks my heart. I've driven by there a hundred times and each time I've said to myself, 'Jake, someday you're gonna do something to help those kids.'"

Tears started to well up in Jake's eyes as Milt whispered to Marty, "Oh, shit. Here we go again."

Jake's voice got louder as he said, "Well, I'm a trucker for retarded kids! And I pledge today that this charity is gonna send one thousand dollars to that school!"

Everyone was cheering and applauding as Jake ran from the stage wiping his eyes with his red scarf. Marty appeared to be sinking under the table but came out in time to try to tackle Bobby Ray Sutton after he grabbed the microphone and announced, "You know, there's a church out there in El Rancho Heights that kept me on the straight and narrow as a kid. It had as much to do with me making it to the PGA as anybody. Well, you can bet that the First Baptist Church of El Rancho Heights is gonna get one thousand dollars of this money for the great work they do with kids!"

Milt simply said to his brother, "Get this thing over with! Punt! We have to stop it now before any more money is pledged or any more celebrities are promised!"

Marty knew there was to be a closing number to the press conference, and as he ran to the back of the room to get it started, Marcus Pauley went to the podium with Marcella Mississippi. Marcus spoke into the microphone. "I'm Marcus Pauley and I grew up in the projects here in Houston. Those kids got it tough there. I'd like to see some money go to those kids in the projects."

Marcella said, "Marcus is right. I grew up in a ghetto and kids in the ghetto have it tough too. So I propose one thousand dollars to ghetto kids." She was then interrupted by Marcus who said, "And kids of the projects," as Marcella said the word, "each." Marcella had meant one thousand dollars each for the projects and the ghetto, but in the confusion it sounded like Marcus and Marcella had pledged one thousand dollars to each kid in the projects and the ghetto.

The taped music to the song "There's No Business Like Show Business" began to play through the show room as Marty rushed back to the podium and said, "Thank you for attending our press conference. We want to thank the Houston press for all of your help. And don't rush off—there is still some food and the bar is still open. Again thanks for supporting The Comics Open!"

With that, Linda Hart proceeded up the aisle of the audience singing, instead of "There's No Business Like Show Business," "There's No Open Like The Comics Open." As she approached the stage waitresses Carolyn and Patty were behind her with Larry Lawrence and they were doing kicks like the Rockettes as Linda sang,

"There's no open like the Comic's Open,
like no open I know.
Everything about it is appealing,
More laughs that you will ever know.
Monies for many charities,
A golf tournament and then a show!"

Every television news show in Houston carried a report about the press conference for The Comics Open at The Comedy Werks. It was shown at four o'clock, at five and six, ten and eleven. The lead-in was always the shot from the news helicopter and the announcer saying, "Stay tuned for the news and we'll tell you why all those people are waving."

There was a shot of Jake Davis waving from his big rig and then a shot of the banner on the side of his truck. The newsperson's opening statement was about the "extremely entertaining news conference held at The Comedy Werks Comedy Club for an upcoming celebrity golf tournament and show for charity."

I watched the news broadcasts with Milt and Marty in their office. There was a shot of the opening sketch with Harry Bosco and the comics playing news reporters. There was a shot of Linda Hart singing—with Patty, Carolyn, and Larry high-kicking behind her. My mom saw me on the news before I did. There was a shot of me at the podium as the newsperson said, "And a message was read from the chief of police."

There were shots of Milt and Marty with the words "Owners of The Comedy Werks" superimposed at the bottom of the screen. The news people explained what the tournament and the show was for and where and when it was going to be held. They talked about how funny the news conference was, as they showed shots of Clay, Barry Stein, and me as Colombo.

They also talked about how touching it was as club owners and comedians pledged to outdo each other in their quest to raise money for the charities. As those statements were being made, there were shots of Hank Bruno crying and then hugging Marcus Pauley. Then there were shots of Bobby Ray and Brenda crying, as well as Steven Reed and Jake Davis.

What Milt, Marty, and I hated the most was the ten-second shot of Mark Silverman at the podium as the announcer said, "And then the celebrities were announced. Jerry Lewis, Buddy Hackett, and Robin Williams will be attending as well as Gabe Kaplan, Jimmie Walker, Billy Crystal, and more from movies and television. Sports heroes Nolan Ryan, Earl Campbell, and Hakeem Olajuwon, as well as Roger Staubach. The really big news was that Willie Nelson will be in the tournament and performing at the show."

The three of us cringed when the news anchor announced, "Many charities will benefit from this event. Pledged a thousand dollars each were the Hartley School for the Handicapped on the outskirts of Houston, El Rancho Heights First Baptist Church, some Jewish charities, and children of the housing projects and the ghetto, just to name a few."

The last shot of the press conference was of Helen Scoggins standing at the podium with tears streaming down her face and saying, "God bless Houston comedy!"

The radio accounts and newspaper articles were just as damaging. The phone started ringing in Milt and Marty's office immediately after the first newscast with people from the handicapped school and Jewish leaders wondering when they could pick up their money. There were also hundreds of calls from inner-city kids wondering when they would get their thousand bucks and if they had to have an ID to prove they lived in the projects or the ghetto.

As it turned out, there were two people who absolutely loved the news accounts of the press conference. Sergeant Harry Herndon was absolutely thrilled to see how completely out of control the event had already become. He hated the Comedy Werks, comedians, and anyone who appeared to be having a good time. But he loved the trouble he sensed we were all headed for.

Sergeant Herndon immediately jumped into his unmarked police car and started driving through the housing projects and ghettos asking the young black kids there, "Have you got your thousand dollars yet? Well, you call The Comedy Werks and then go over and pick it up. Y'all got it coming."

The other was Packy Hester, a drug dealer who specialized in the show business industry. Anyone who worked at or performed in a honky tonk, comedy club or any other entertainment venue in Southern Texas had seen Packy Hester at least once.

I'll bet his eyes cleared up for a moment and the fog lifted from his brain. Packy probably stopped loading Baggies and mixing chemicals when he saw the accounts on television of the news conference. He was extremely excited about an event that would bring together that many comedians, groupies, bar personnel, and comedy fans. Packy thought The Comics Open might be his biggest drug-selling event since the Rolling Stones came to Houston.

CHAPTER SIX

Reaction to the press conference was swift. At least it was for me. My phone rang off the hook and that was just my mom. She felt obliged to call me every time a friend or relative mentioned to her they had seen me on the news. Her message was always, "I am so proud of you." And, "You should stand up straighter."

I never really understood the power of television until then. I heard from two old girlfriends who had seen me on the news as well as my dentist, my car mechanic and assorted college buddies, one of whom used his accounting degree to go into the world or illegal bookmaking. He asked me, "Dale, this Comics Open—is it the kind of golf tournament one could take bets on?"

My answer was, "No, unless you want to take bets on how many people get hit by stray golf balls and how many people go to the emergency room. If you can get action on that, take the over."

I got a kick out of hearing from all the people I knew who saw me on television but there was one person I didn't enjoy hearing from. I was at the police department to see Dad when Sergeant Herndon stopped me in a hallway. "Saw you on the news cracking jokes with all of your degenerate friends. No way for the son of the chief to act. But I was happy to hear the news about The Comics Open. Stay clear, that's where I plan on getting them all. Out in the open at The Comics Open."

I was surprised at how mild he was, and it gave me a chill that he was so calm and he had the most devilish smile. It wasn't like the last time he confronted me about The Comedy Werks and the people who performed there. That time I thought his head was going to explode right in front of me.

Harold Herndon was a forty-seven-year-old sergeant who had been passed over for the position of lieutenant three times. He had red, curly hair, was overweight, and always seemed to be sweating. He turned red whenever he got mad and almost everything pissed off Harry Herndon.

His wife's name was Loretta and I had met her and their twin daughters at a department picnic. A dispatcher had told me she used to baby-sit those girls and their interests were the same as their mother's—eating, watching television, and going to church. The girls were now twenty-five years old, still living at home, and still eating, watching television, and going to church with their mother.

It was Harry's wife's idea that they should go to The Comedy Werks after she read a nice article about Milt and Marty and what went on at The Comedy Werks. Loretta thought it would be like an evening with The Brady Bunch. It turned out to be more like an evening with The Addams Family.

I don't know why I hid when I saw the Herndons walk into The Comedy Werks that night but I'm glad I did. I found a spot behind the bar where I could observe every-thing. Their evening was highlighted by Larry Lawrence telling Harry he had "clenched hair" and his "sport coat looks like the horse blanket for the Grand Marshal of the Gay Pride Parade."

When Harry started to turn a record shade of red, Larry said, "Look how red he's getting! I recognize you now! You're the camp counselor who molested me fifteen years ago! Oh, how I've missed you!"

Larry said of the fur wrap that Loretta was wearing around her neck, "Let me guess. When your schnauzer died and you couldn't bear to let him go, you had him skinned and you are now wearing him around your neck."

Harry and Loretta were running for the backdoor as Marcella Mississippi was introduced. She took the microphone, pointed at Loretta, and said of the dress she was wearing, "That woman is wearing my bedspread! That white lady is my maid and she stole my bedspread and she's wearing it right now!"

Harry and Loretta were in full gallop and the last thing they heard before they burst through the backdoor into a cloud of marijuana smoke was Marcella screaming, "Where are you going, maid? To give your man a blow job in the parking lot?"

I thought Sergeant Herndon was going to explode when he told me of that experience and he swore he was going to take The Comedy Werks down. He knew The Comedy Werks was to the comics what Sherwood Forest was to Robin Hood and his Merry Men. He knew he could never get them on their own turf. But the comics were coming out for The Comics Open. He must have laughed when he saw that there was even a press conference to announce it.

It was strange to have a member of the police department swearing he was going to take down The Comics Open. I tried to think of the worst thing he could do to us. He couldn't go to my dad or any of his superiors because the department was officially behind The Comics Open. I figured that the only thing he could do was come up with a drug charge and go to the district attorney or the newspapers with it.

The news coverage of the press conference got the promotion for The Comics Open off to an excellent start; then it was up to the board of directors, the comics, the sponsors, and the comedy clubs to keep it rolling. The emcees of each of the comedy clubs encouraged their audience members every night to buy Comics Open T-shirts and tickets to the golf tournament, as well as tickets to the show afterwards. The show was touted as "the greatest comedy show in the history of Houston." Bumper stickers were also sold at the comedy clubs and no audience member was allowed to leave without one. The bumper stickers read "I Support The Comics Open June 17. The Funniest Charity in Houston."

Most of the radio DJs in town were promised that they would be able to play in the tournament so they kept the airwaves filled with that information. "I'll be playing in The Comics Open at The El Rancho Heights Golf Course June 17! That event ought to be like The Marx Brothers meet the PGA!"

Deveraux Clay Clayton was interviewed on one radio station and described what he thought the upcoming Comics Open would be like, "Imagine Woodstock but as a golf tournament."

The biggest promotion on the radio was not by the comics or even the DJs, but by a song. A favorite local rock band of some of the comedians got to partying and jamming one night after a gig and came up with a song called "The Comics Open." They got some free studio time and recorded it the next day—all within a thirty-six hour period without any sleep.

The group was a former shrimp boat crew that went by the name of Big Shrimpy and The Crabs. I thought the song was great and even my mother liked it. It was an upbeat tune and my favorite part was:

"If life is getting you down
and you're having trouble copin',
Then come along with me to The Comics Open.
The money is for charity
But the laughs are for free,
Let's go to The Comics Open—come along with me."

They printed thousands on cassette tapes and promoted the song on radio, selling the tapes for five bucks a piece. All of that money went to the charity, and Big Shrimpy and The Crabs said during one radio interview, "We're just glad we could contribute." They were disappointed that they weren't allowed to put their underground classic on the tape, "I'm Leaving You Now But I'll Be Back When You're 18."

Alex Day got a quote in one of Houston's major newspapers when he described what he thought The Open would be like in a section called "Quotable Quotes," in which famous people from around the country and Houston were quoted on any and all subjects. The last paragraph of that section one Monday morning read, "Houston comedian Alex Day described the charity golf tournament and show, called The Comics Open, that will take place June 17: 'It will be just like the U.S. Congress—it will be a big mess. But the difference will be that it will be funny and a lot of good will come out of it.'"

The official board of directors–approved promo photo of The Comics Open was showing up everywhere. It was in newspapers and magazines, and even on the cover of *The Houston Golfer.* The picture was of the board of directors, each of whom was holding a crippled child. And next to Milt in his wheelchair was a child smiling in her wheelchair. In the row behind that child was Helen Scoggins and the representatives of the official sponsors of The Comics Open.

I was one of about thirty comedians in that photo-graph and we were all holding golf clubs or microphones and most of us were making funny faces. I thought it was a pretty good picture, especially because only three of the comics appeared to be giving the finger.

Milt told me, "That's how we decided on that picture over the other twenty-three pictures that were taken. It had the least amount of comedians giving the finger. The bastards."

Milt and Marty used the media not only to promote The Comics Open but also to do some damage control. Milt's basic message on seven radio interviews and one television show was: "In all of the excitement some people and different organizations were promised money from this and it's just not possible to give to everybody. And some celebrities names were thrown around as if they were going to play in the tournament and perform in the show; but they won't be necessary, because our very own Houston comedians and comics from around the state and even the country will be more than enough entertain-ment."

Even with his disclaimers, Milt and his brother Marty continued to receive phone calls from people they didn't even know who said they were promised money from The Comics Open. And there were the continuous visits from the children of the ghetto and projects who wondered when they could pick up their thousand dollars. One day Milt got fed up with it and hung up on a man who asked, "Is Johnny Cash playing in the tournament *and* singing in the show, or just singing in the show?"

Another person who was filling the airwaves with the message of The Comics Open was the Trucker Comic, Jake Davis. Jake didn't need radio or television to be heard because he had his own CB radio. He was criss-crossing the state of Texas inviting fellow truckers to attend or at least buy a Comic's Open T-shirt. "Come on, all you truckers! This is the Trucker Comic Jake Davis inviting y'all to attend The Comics Open and show, June 17 in El Rancho Heights, Houston. All the money goes to retarded kids. I need y'all to buy a Comics Open T-shirt from me or any comedy club in the state for seven dollars. And if you wear that T-shirt to the tournament or the show then you can get your picture taken with me and Willie Nelson!"

There was a "Comics Open" banner displayed prominently at all of the Astros home games at the Astrodome. No less than six comics and/or comedy club personnel were at each game, parading their twenty-foot by five-foot banner around the stadium. It was very visible, and even my dad and one of my uncles told me how many times they had seen it on TV or when they were at a game.

The comedians would drink beer and parade their banner around, every once in a while draping the banner in a prominent place and taking a break. And that was when the trouble started. Once the comics draped their banner over the right field wall over one that said "Jesus Saves" and one with the biblical passage "John 3:16."

The young men who had displayed the religious banners tried to remove the "Comics Open" banner off of theirs and that's when Billy Meyer decided to give them a baptism with his glass of beer. Billy threw it on three of them and got knocked down for his trouble. As he said later, "I guess turning the other cheek doesn't apply to beer."

It must have been a slow baseball game because the radio announcer alluded to the problem in the right field bleachers between The Comics Open guys and the evangelical guys. After describing the thrown beer and Billy being knocked down, the announcer said, "I would have to score the altercation as evangelical Christians, one. Comedians, zero."

A highlight for me, and especially my mother, was when I was picked to accompany Milt and Marty on the *Good Morning, Houston* television show with hosts Bonnie Praline and Lance Childress. My mom watched that show religiously and I knew all of our relatives and neighbors would be watching.

The three of us were introduced and the studio audience gave us a nice round of applause as I walked out behind Marty who was pushing Milt in his wheelchair. Marty didn't say much but Milt did and he even gave me credit for the idea of The Comics Open. I did my mom's favorite impression, which was Edith Bunker saying, "Don't have sauerkraut on your hot dog at the ball game, Archie. You know sauerkraut gives you gas." And my dad's favorite, which was Don Knotts as Barney Fife saying, "Drink and drive and you'll hear the big door slam."

The show was running smoothly until Milt, who appeared to be at least a little hung over, started to get annoyed with Bonnie Praline. In the past he had cracked some jokes onstage saying, "What a phony she is. She made one B movie in Hollywood and she is introduced every morning on *Good Morning, Houston* as, 'The Hollywood movie actress, Bonnie Praline.'"

"I have been to The Comedy Werks once," Bonnie commented, "and I must say that your show is not for the faint of heart."

Milt came back with, "Bonnie, some nights our show is like that one movie you made in Hollywood. For the people watching it, it is nothing more than a form of punishment."

My mom loved the show and the phone calls started again.

Promoting the tournament and show opened up a little television work for some of the comics in Houston. The cable access channel always used local comedians on interview shows and commercials to publicize upcoming community events, although the comics weren't paid for their services. However, comics always got a kick out of it and also felt obliged to do certain commercials like the fund-raising drives for the Houston Free Clinics. Because, like Clay said at the press conference, the comics felt they probably were the ones who used the free clinics' services the most.

Barry Stein talked the cable access channel into running a seven-second commercial he taped himself. The commercial, which ran a lot, was of Barry holding a driver and standing on a tee box with a ball teed up. Behind him was a majorette from a local high school, who was twirling two golf clubs over her head as Barry said into the camera, "Attend and support The Comics Open Golf Tournament and show in El Rancho Heights June 17! You'll get a big bang out of it!" He then swung the club and hit an exploding golf ball.

Some of the comedians wanted me to ask my dad if they could borrow a police car and a cop for a commercial. They wanted the cop to handcuff a comic and as he put the comic into the back seat of the patrol car, the cop says, "Don't worry, you'll be out in time for The Comics Open and show on June 17." I didn't even bother asking my dad because I knew he wouldn't go for it.

I did get to be in a commercial with my dad and a clown. The clown was juggling behind my dad who was sitting at his desk. I was standing next to my dad wearing one of those red, fuzzy balls on the end of my nose as my dad said into the camera, "The Houston Police Department supports The Comics Open and show on June 17—and that's no joke." Again, my mother was proud to see me on television and she commented on how good my posture was.

There were some comedians who started getting paid to do television commercials for some of the sponsors of the tournament. Linda Hart and three other comics got hired to do commercials for the supermarket chain sponsor. The executives for the chain absolutely loved Linda but despised the three other comics who showed up with her: Chad Stevens, Harry Bosco, and Daryl Reese.

They were improvisational players and funny at first, going through the supermarket acting like a combination of The Three Stooges and The Bowery Boys. Things went bad when the comics started eating and then shoplifting some of the store's products. Chad was juggling some fruit and vegetables, while Harry stood next to him eating a banana. Harry then shook up a liter of soda, took the top off, and sprayed it into the camera, as he screamed, "Support The Comics Open or we're coming to your homes!"

While all that was going on, Daryl was in the meat section stuffing a four-pound steak down the front of his pants. A stock boy informed the assistant manager what Daryl had done, and she confronted him in front of the store executives and commercial camera crew asking him, "Is that a big piece of meat you have inside the front of your pants?"

Daryl answered through a wide smile, "Yes, and thanks for noticing."

Daryl, Chad, and Harry never did get paid for their efforts and none of what they did ever made it to television as a commercial or a promotion for The Comics Open, but Linda Hart did very well, not only in promoting The Open, but by developing her own career. Linda did song parodies and was seen on television, singing and dancing down the aisles of that supermarket. She soon became the spokeswoman for the chain and solidified her position by having an affair, first with the regional manager of the chain, and then with the president of the company.

On a smaller scale Brenda, Greg Okada, Brent Harris, and Bobby Sanchez got to do a local commercial for a dry cleaners, thanks to Brent. A friend of his owned three dry cleaners in the black neighborhoods of Houston and Brent talked him into supporting The Open and doing some television commercials starring himself and his three friends.

Everyone's favorite commercial was the one with Brent acting as the spokesman and talking about how great all three of Johnson's Cleaners were and how great it was that Johnson's Cleaners was to be one of the cosponsors of The Comics Open. Brent then said, "At Johnson's we serve everybody," as he pushed a button starting the machine that brings around the clean clothes. On the machine, as if they were each an item of clothing, hung Brenda, Greg, and then Bobby, as Brent said, "We serve Caucasians, Asians, and Mexicans." The last words of the commercial were Bobby saying, "*Se habla español.*"

Brent, Brenda, Greg, and Bobby got a year's worth of free dry cleaning services for doing those commercials, and that's how the trouble slowly but surely got started. The comedians of Houston were a very competitive lot and they got jealous when they saw that some of their peers were receiving goods and services from some of the sponsors and they weren't. At first they didn't think they too could cash in with the sponsors, but things got completely out of control when the comedians realized they could cash in big—if they got their own sponsors.

CHAPTER SEVEN

As the fateful day approached, I started to notice signs in small-to-medium-size businesses as I drove around the city. Most were homemade signs that said, "Official Sponsor of The Comics Open." My gut told me that something was going on so I started going into those businesses to see what was happening.

I would congratulate the store owner or manager on being an official sponsor of The Comics Open, then ask, "What does that entail?" and, "Who approached you about being a sponsor?"

The answers didn't surprise me at all and they were always just about the same. "Some of the comedians from the local comedy club came in," they said. "They told us about the tremendous charity work they were doing and how we could help with the donation of some of our products or services."

I finally hit on where the whole thing got started—Big Al's Big and Tall Store. I thought that name was fitting because that is where the bullshit started to stack up mighty big and very tall.

Big Al had more of a banner than a homemade sign and that was what caught my attention. I entered his store and we got to talking and he explained how it all happened.

"A couple of the comedians came in—big guys. One was a former football player named Honeycutt. The other was half of a comedy team. Nice guys who say I'll have a nice sign displayed at the golf tournament and a space in the program at the show afterwards."

It was Big Bill Blevens and a comic friend of his from Tulsa by the name of Buddy Honeycutt who had played right guard for the Oklahoma State football team. Buddy lived in Tulsa because he had a job there at the radio station, but he hung around Houston a lot to do standup comedy and he was in town for the tournament and show. Bill and Buddy had taken their wide bodies into Big Al's and before they left they were both wearing plush jogging suits and carrying bags with slacks, shirts, and sweaters for the tournament. Their double-breasted suits were to be ready in time to wear in the show, all free of charge.

Bill and Buddy wore their fancy jogging suits into The Comedy Werks that night and bragged about how they got clothes for the tournament and suits that would be ready to wear for the show. They also stopped into three of the other comedy clubs because Buddy wanted to make the rounds and see some friends, and they bragged about how they got their new clothes at each club. That was the beginning of the pillaging of Houston.

All of the comics got new clothes. If they hit a store that had already given to some other comics, then they thanked them for their support and moved on to another store. They got golf clubs, golf bags, golf balls, and golf shoes, and Alex Lewis even got a pair of snow skis, poles, and boots.

When the man at the sporting goods store asked Alex what skiing equipment could possibly have to do with a charity golf tournament, Alex replied, "There's a kid at the crippled children's hospital who is my exact same size and he told me that, before he dies, he wants to snow ski. You and I have a chance to make his last wish come true."

Marcus Pauley got a boombox he said was for the tournament, but a stereo for his car was a hard sell. He told the stereo store owner, "I will be picking up Charlie Pride at the airport and then driving him to his hotel, the tournament, the show, and back. He'll be spending a lot of time in my car and I don't want him listening to music on anything less than one of your stereos." He ended up with the top-of-the-line model.

Music stores got hit the hardest and they were all promised an exclusive at the tournament and show. The only thing that would have been an exclusive for a music store would have been if one of them got left out, but that didn't happen. The most interesting promise to a music store was made to Lone Star Music when Harry Bosco said, "Willie Nelson's caddy will be wearing a one- foot by one-foot patch on his back with Lone Star Music embroidered on it."

They couldn't get booze by the bottle, but they finagled gift certificates to their favorite restaurants and bars. They didn't get the televisions they wanted, but they got many services donated to them, including car tune-ups, oil changes, and wheel alignments. They got passes to movies and theme parks. They even got free haircuts.

Marcella Mississippi couldn't get the fur coat she wanted and she was disappointed when she couldn't get a leather jacket. But she did end up getting something she didn't even ask for, which was a gown from the department store where she tried to get the coats.

Marcella had never worn a gown before. She had never gone to her junior prom in high school or the senior ball or the graduation night party. She had never even been in a wedding. The store donated a gown to Marcella to wear in the show after the tournament and the only stipulation was, "When people ask you where you got it, be sure to tell them."

The gown looked like a purple wedding dress and it even had a bit of a train. It had puffed shoulders and came up to her neck but was cut down to her waist in the back. It had purple sequins and shimmered in the dark. When Marcella tried it on she just stared into the mirror at herself for the longest time, like she didn't recognize the person she was looking at. She couldn't wait to wear the gown in the show. Marcella told me, "Dale, when some women get dolled up it's said they can stop traffic. Well, what I'm wearing to the show after the tournament could close down an airport."

Larry Lawrence lobbied the gay community of Houston hard for their support. He wanted them to buy tickets for the tournament and show and donate whatever services they could. Those donated services were only taken advantage of by other gay men, because no straight men were going to go into a gay bar for a free lunch, nor were they going to get their hair cut for free at a place called The Manhole.

The most ingenious scam of all was pulled off by Barry Stein, the prop comic, and his roommate David Luben, who was an open-miker, Monday night comic. David's father owned a sign store and they had four signs made up. They were plastic signs with magnets that could be stuck on to doors of cars and trucks for a company to advertise their product or service.

They then went over to Sanders Ford Lincoln Mercury of Houston and asked to see Mr. Sanders. When Will Sanders came out to see them in the show room, they had already put their four signs on the four doors of a brand new, cream-colored Lincoln Town Car. On the two front doors the signs read, "Official Car of The Comics Open." On the two backdoors the signs said, "Donated by Will Sanders of Sanders Ford Lincoln Mercury of Houston."

Will Sanders, who was an old friend of my dad's, explained to me what happened. "They were very cordial young men. The one said, 'Mr. Sanders, we came to you first. Is the answer yes, or do we have to make up two new signs for the backdoors?'"

"You let them have a car?" I said, trying to hide my shock.

"I had to go for it," Mr. Sanders explained. "It's for charity, but I agree with the boys that the celebrities should be picked up in something nice at the airport. I have to admit that it's also good business, because they promised me I would be introduced at the show—and at least one of the celebrities will do a commercial with me. I can't decide between Jerry Lewis, Robin Williams, Willie Nelson, or Charlie Pride."

I didn't say anything. I don't think I could have if I wanted to. Mr. Sanders continued, "At first I was against letting them have the car two weeks before the tournament, but when they told me it was to drive the crippled children around the city to news conferences and television shows, I changed my mind in a hurry. God bless those boys for the work they are doing."

Barry and David pulled up in front of The Comedy Werks that night and, before they got out of the car, almost all of us comics, bar personnel, and even Milt and Marty were out on the

sidewalk staring at it. Everyone was laughing except for Milt and Marty and when everybody finally settled down, Milt said, "I know what you've been doing and this car is the biggest example of it yet. All I can say is you better start hustling some lawyers for some free legal work, because I think we're all going to need it."

Milt looked at me for help so I gave my best attempt at a warning. "You probably haven't done anything illegal yet but you sure are misrepresenting yourselves. The charity is not for us comics—" I tried to go on but was interrupted by some of the comedians.

"The company line! You're starting to sound like a supervisor, Dale!"

And, "Hey, Dale! You're not going to tell your dad, are you?"

Milt knew he had put me between a rock and a hard place so he came to my rescue by saying "Forget it!" as he wheeled himself back inside the club.

I felt like I was in no man's land. I was still a comic but I wasn't one hundred percent with them and I wasn't on board of directors or the planning committee. I was neither fish nor fowl. I was in the crummy, impossible position of trying to ask the comedians to behave.

Clay was the only comedian who seemed to notice my predicament. He asked me, "Dale, what's the road to hell paved with?"

"Good intentions," was my snap answer.

"Yeah," said Clay, laughing. "You've got good intentions. You're like that prime minister of England who came back from Germany with a piece of paper signed by Hitler saying he wouldn't start a world war. Nice idea and it probably made that prime minister feel real good, until Hitler started World War II anyway."

I said to Clay, "So I'm like that prime minister that went down in history as an idiot?"

"No," Clay said. "Come to think of it, your idea for The Comics Open is more like that Chinese guy who invented gun powder. He thought it was going to be used for fireworks, to entertain people and especially children. He didn't know that his idea was going to end up killing more people than any other idea in history."

"Thanks, Clay," I said. "I feel better knowing that I not only got a bad idea but that bad idea is going to make me famous."

"Just in Houston," Clay said through his laughter. "You're just going to be known as an idiot in Houston."

"Great," I said sarcastically. "That's just great."

As it turned out, the Lincoln Town car that Barry and David got was not the biggest example of the pillaging that was going on. The Monday before the tournament, I was on the freeway when I was passed by an eighteen wheeler. I couldn't believe my eyes when I saw the truck, so I pulled up along the driver's side of it and saw that it was Jake Davis, The Trucker Comic. Jake had taken the two Comics Open banners off his trailer and replaced them with two big banners that read "Red Haskins' Texaco Truck Stop." Under that it read "The Official Truck Stop of The Comics Open."

Jake Davis had outdone every other comic when it came to procuring goods and services for himself in the name of The Comics Open. Jake had talked Red Haskins into a complete engine overhaul on his truck, which would have cost Jake around a thousand dollars. Jake told Red to buy a couple of big banners to put on the sides of his trailer so all of Houston would know about the great work Red Haskins was doing.

Many of the comedians made jokes onstage about Red Haskins' television commercials. "Red Haskins is what happens when cousins marry," was one joke I could remember. Another one was, "Red Haskins should be on the cover of *White Trash* magazine." I noticed that Red Haskins spoke better on the commercials with his teeth out as opposed to when he had them in.

"Fine man, that Jake Davis," Red Haskins said to me the day I went out to talk to him. "I admire the work he and all of the comedians are doing. I'm proud to put my name on something so good. Jake said everyone would see the banners on his truck and he would park it prominently at the golf tournament and in front of the high school where they are going to have the show."

I asked Red if there was anything else and he shook his head and said, "Maybe I just should have gone ahead and given Jake those eighteen new tires he wants for his truck, but I told him let's see how it goes. If you have another tournament next year, then we'll see about those tires."

Red Haskins added something that gave me a chill. "Everything is on the up and up with this charity, isn't it? I mean, you are the second guy to come out here and talk to me about it. The other was a sergeant with the Houston Police Department."

I lied and told Red that everything was on the up and up. Even if the comics could get away with everything, I knew there was someone who was going to make sure they didn't. Red Haskins wasn't the first person who had mentioned someone else had been around because three business owners had told me that they "had already talked to a sergeant."

I knew what was going on. Sergeant Herndon was gathering evidence and taking notes and going about his investigation. I even watched him one night through a window at The Comedy Werks as he sat in his car and watched the comedians in the back parking lot. He watched the comics open the trunks of their cars and start swinging brand new golf clubs and try on new clothes that still had the price tags on them. He watched as Alex Lewis tried on a new pair of ski boots and skis.

I knew that Sergeant Herndon could possibly take down The Comedy Werks without even trying to make it a police matter. All he had to do was take it to a newspaper and the story would be devastating. The story would be about how the comedians of Houston procured goods and services for themselves illegally in the name of Children's Charities. And the whole thing just happened to be the idea of the son of the chief of police.

But Sergeant Herndon was being smart and biding his time. What he was really waiting and hoping for was something flagrant that he could arrest someone for. Harry Herndon was waiting for the big bust.

CHAPTER EIGHT

It was three days before the tournament and I was driving along wondering what was going to happen next when I saw the biggest set of tits I had ever seen. Then I saw a second set. They were sticking out of the side windows of a car that had honked at me as it passed me going the other way. I made a U-turn and eventually pulled alongside of the cream colored Town Car for another look, and that's when I saw the signs on the doors. I noticed that David Luben was driving when another set of tits stuck out of the window accompanied by Billy Meyer's head.

I shook my head at them and as I murmured to myself, "The boys are at it again," I followed them to The Comedy Werks.

It was almost two-thirty in the morning when we all arrived in front of the club. There were some comics standing out in front of the club and when they saw the Town Car they hollered inside for everyone to come out. Alex Lewis said later, "It was like that thing in the circus when the car pulls up and about a hundred clowns get out. Well, a lot of clowns got out of this car, but so did a lot of topless dancers."

The comics' getting goods and services in the name of charity was wrong and to say that celebrities were going to attend The Comics Open and show was a complete lie. But all of that paled in comparison when the comics started interviewing young women for a fictitious title they called "Queen of The Comics Open."

It had to happen and no one particular comic thought of it—it was as if they all did. A comic would be coming on to a young lady and when he saw that the conversation wasn't going anywhere, he would hear himself say, "Have you heard about The Comics Open? You ought to try out for Queen of The Comics Open. I'll bet you've been in beauty pageants before."

They tried that line on women in comedy clubs, at the bars they went to, and everywhere else they went. They tried that line on all kinds of women, from the most wholesome of young ladies, to the girls who worked in titty bars. "You should try out for the Queen of The Comics Open. There's money, prizes, and a cruise to the Bahamas for you. I think you could win because I'm on the panel of judges."

I got bits and pieces of information from all seven of the guys involved and I wasn't the least bit surprised to hear how it happened. That Wednesday night before the tournament, Clay, Billy Meyer, Greg Okada, Brent Harris, and Bobby Sanchez all piled into "The Official Car of The Comics Open" with Barry Stein and David Luben and attempted to hit every titty bar in Houston. They had it all worked out. They would pass themselves off as the official panel of judges in search of a queen for The Comics Open. They had the Lincoln Town Car with the official signs on the sides and their plan was to take each contestant for a ride in the car as part of their interview.

They first went to a place called The Crazy Kitten, and then its sister club across the street, The Crimson

Kitten. They stopped in places called The Purple Booty, The Pleasure Parade, Satin Doll, and Hootarama's.

Most of the dancers took stage names after their favorite male celebrities. Instead of John Travolta, they saw Jan Travolta, as well as Paula McCartney and Paula Newman. Some of the girls must have been sports fans because they had names like Nola Ryan, Doctor Jay, and there was a tiny little dancer who must have been a horse race fan because her name was Willy "The Shoe" Shoemaker.

Barry Stein's favorite was the one introduced at the Purple Booty as "Roberta DeNiro as Jake LaMotta, the Raging Bull!" She came out dancing wearing nothing but a boxer's robe that said "The Raging Bull" on the back of it.

There were three very large and big-busted black girls at The Purple Booty who all took the names of sports celebrities. There was Houston's very own heavyweight champ, Georgia Foreman. There was the pride of the Oilers, Erla Campbell, and visiting from Dallas, Edna "Too Tall" Jones.

It was while they were at The Purple Booty they first encountered the woman who was to be their queen. The emcee announced, "And now, from Columbus, Ohio, that legend of the links, the Golden Bear, Jackie Nicklaus!'

All seven of the comics stood up as a big-busted, middle-aged woman came out wearing nothing but black and white golf shoes, without the spikes, and a gold G-string. On the nipples of her giant breasts she had white tassels, which looked exactly like two golf balls. She had golden hair and a big smile and as she danced she twirled a golf club in each hand over her head and twirled the golf ball tassels in opposite directions. "That's her!" the seven comics screamed. "That's our queen!"

Jackie "The Golden Bear" Nicklaus was probably confused at first, but her basic attitude seemed to be, "It's great to win anything." She loved the big fuss that was being made over her and was especially impressed when the boys started ordering champagne.

Clay explained "the tremendous honor" that had been bestowed upon her and some of the duties she would have to perform. He also informed her that she would have "a court of six other women," which just happened to be the number of guys Clay had with him. Jackie set Barry Stein up with his favorite girl, who was Roberta DeNiro as Jake LaMotta, "The Raging Bull."

Brent Harris got the very large black girl named Erla Campbell. Greg Okada got Nola Ryan, and Bobby Sanchez got a Hispanic girl by the name of Viva Zapata. Everyone figured that Billy Meyer would want the tiny Willie "The Shoe" Shoemaker but he surprised them all when he said to Jackie in a firm voice, "Edna 'Too Tall' Jones."

Jackie rounded out her court by introducing Dave Luben to her bartender and dancer friend, by the name of Elva Presley. Elva was also an Elvis impersonator and when David said to her, "Nice to meet you," she replied as Elvis, "Thank you very much."

None of the seven women had any reservations about leaving after closing and riding over to The Comedy Werks to meet the chairman of the board and to make the whole thing official. Clay insisted they all ride in the official car of The Comics Open. The girls got their things, and as they all walked out the front door, David Luben pointed at the Lincoln Town Car and said, "Your chariot awaits."

Fourteen people are a lot even for a Lincoln Town Car, but Jackie described it as "a fun fit." David Luben drove, as he sat on the lap of Elva Presley, and next to them was Bobby Sanchez, who was holding Viva Zapata. Riding shotgun was Clay who had seemed to disappear when Jackie sat on him.

The back seat was a sea of laughter and large breasts. Erla Campbell was sitting in the middle on the lap of Brent and next to them and the window was Billy who was sitting on the lap of Edna "Too Tall" Jones. Erla yelled to the front seat, "Look! An Oreo cookie!" When everyone turned and looked they saw Billy's face squished between the giant black breasts of Erla and Edna.

Greg Okada was sitting on the floor at Edna's feet with his back up against the door, while he was holding Nola Ryan who was sitting between his legs. Greg had to be somewhat uncomfortable physically because of his position; but if he was, his face certainly didn't show it. Greg had a smile from ear to ear.

Sitting at the other back window was Barry Stein with Roberta DeNiro on his lap. Roberta kept doing lines from the movie *Raging Bull* that kept Barry in stitches. "Look at these hands," she said to Barry, as Jake La Motta, as she showed him her fists. "Little girl hands. It means no matter how good I get. I'll never be able to fight Joe Louis." Barry's favorite moment on the ride was when Roberta told him, "The only part of the film I couldn't relate to was when Jake said, 'I don't go down for nobody.' That's just not me."

In the front seat, Bobby was speaking Spanish with Viva, and when Clay saw me in my car, coming the other way, all those tits were flashed out the window at me.

Steven Reed described the entrance of Erla Campbell: "Her tits got out of the car about five seconds before she did."

Clay gave Alex Lewis Jackie's tape and told him to turn it on when he signaled. He also told him to tell Milt and Marty and everybody else there to sit in the audience and hold onto their hats. Clay asked me to walk in first and then Clay walked in by himself. When he saw that Milt, Marty, the bar staff and twenty comics and hangers-on were all seated, he yelled the announcement, "Ladies and gentlemen! I give you the Queen of The Comics Open, Jackie, 'The Golden Bear' Nicklaus!"

With that, Clay motioned to Alex to hit the tape and the music began. Jackie danced her way on to the stage dressed the same as she was at her club, gold G-string, white golf ball tassels on her nipples, while twirling two golf clubs over her head. Clay then joined her onstage and as he grabbed the microphone he said, "Now I would like to introduce the queen's court! First, the pride of Houston, Erla Campbell!" Erla danced her way to the stage and gyrated to the music, as she occasionally bared her breasts from beneath a waist-length jacket she was wearing.

Clay continued, "The Express! Nola Ryan!" Nola, too, danced onto the stage and flashed her tits beneath her Astro's baseball shirt. "Viva Zapata!" yelled Clay, as Viva danced her way to the stage. "Roberta DeNiro in her Academy Award winning role, *Raging Bull!*" Roberta went onstage like a fighter going into the ring. Once there, she threw some punches and flashed her tits. Elva Presley was introduced next and she did some of Elvis' best-known gyrations. "Let's have a special welcome," yelled Clay, "for our visitor from Dallas! Edna 'Too Tall' Jones!" Edna went onstage, took off her Dallas Cowboy football jersey, and outdid the rest, as she twirled her huge breasts to the music in one direction and then in the other.

Clay was really proud of himself and played it like a circus ringmaster. He yelled one last time: "Ladies and gentlemen! I give you The Comics Open queen and her court!" Everyone in the room went wild, except for the waitresses, Patty and Carolyn, who looked annoyed. Milt and Marty didn't laugh, but they did have to smile, as I did. We had to admit that Clay and those comics had outdone themselves and the visual images of those top-less dancers, dancing on The Comedy Werks stage, would live on in their memories forever.

The music and dancing didn't stop and Marty okayed some champagne for the queen and her court. Edna kept dancing with Billy who came right up to her breasts. Carolyn and Patty danced with each other in the back of the show room mocking the topless dancers who were onstage. Everyone in the audience was dancing and I just had a beer and watched it all.

Milt, Marty and I went to the quietest part of the show room to talk. They looked back at the stage again, only to hear Erla Campbell scream, "Oreo cookie!" She and Edna then pressed Billy's head between their big black breasts.

Milt took a big swig of beer and then said to his brother, "Marty, you were right and I was wrong. You told me this thing could get too big for us, get out of control, and cause us nothing but trouble, but I didn't listen." Milt then looked at me and said, "The dumbest thing I have ever said in my life, or the dumbest thing ever said in history, was when I said, 'Don't worry, I can control the comedians.'"

Milt took another swig of beer and continued. "Who knows what's going to happen Monday? They might have a parade with all those topless girls on a float, waving to the good people of Houston, and flapping their tits at all of the boys." Marty and I laughed again and this time Marty grabbed his forehead like he'd eaten ice cream too fast. Marty finally said to his brother, "Milty, the way things are going that will probably happen."

I thought of something and offered it up to Milt and Marty. "Who's to say Larry Lawrence isn't out right now organizing a gay marching band?"

"Yeah!" said Milt excitedly. "They'll be marching in front of the float with the topless girls. All the members of the marching band will be naked except for cowboy hats and boots. At one point the leader will give a command and the front line will stop abruptly and they will all rear end each other and commence fucking each other in the butt."

Marty grabbed his head again and laughed uncontrollably. "The news cameras will get it all," Milt went on. "They will cut away from the dancers' tits and the gays' butt-fucking, just to show a logo of ours saying, 'Brought to you by The Comedy Werks' and then they'll go back to tits and butt-fucking."

Marty and I had tears in our eyes from laughter. Marty said, "You're right, we're doomed. They'll think of anything and do anything. Our world comes to an end Monday. Dale, you've got to have access to a gun. Get your dad's revolver for me, would you?"

"You can have it when I'm done with it," I answered seriously. "When my dad realizes what I got him into, I'll be a dead man."

"At the very least you'll be out of the will," added Milt.

"You tried, Marty," Milt went on. "You did as much damage control as anybody ever could have. I heard you take hundreds of calls from those little kids from the ghetto and projects and tell them it was a mistake about them getting a thousand bucks each. You were so nice on the phone and patient with them and everybody else who called wanting money or demanding shit that they had been promised by the comics. I never could have done what you have done."

Marty nodded in a gesture of thanks, as Milt took another swig of beer and continued. "But I did take one phone call. Some girl who sounded about thirteen years old wanted to know how old you have to be to be the queen or a member of her court. I thought, shit, this was the first I heard about the queen and the court thing. So this maybe fourteen-year-old says to me, 'My mom said I have to be eighteen, but the comedian told me I didn't.'"

Marty and I stopped smiling and Milt said, "So I said to her, which comedian? What's his name? And the girl says, 'I don't know, but he works at The Comedy Werks, so I called you.'"

Marty and I both shook our heads as we said simultaneously, "It's really getting bad."

Milt took another swig of beer and said to Marty, "Brother, I think we're going to hell."

Marty just stared at the conga line that had formed and was dancing its way toward us. He finally said to his brother, "No, Milt, I don't think we're going to hell. But we are probably going to jail."

"I'll probably being going to jail too," I said. "But it won't be the same jail as yours because they wouldn't put the son of the chief of police in with the general jail population."

Marty felt better when Jackie stepped out of the conga line and danced up to Milt and said, "Clay says I'm not officially the queen until I do this." With that she started swinging her breasts in Milt's face and rubbing them around until his face seemed to disappear into her chest. Marty knew they were in a lot of trouble, but he felt as he always did—it was worth it as long as his brother was happy. And at that particular moment, Milt looked very happy.

CHAPTER NINE

We were two days away and I started to feel like being a part of The Comics Open was like standing in front of a dam, waiting for it to give way. There was just a slow trickle but things were steadily getting worse. I felt like that little kid with his finger in the dike. I felt the pressure of being the only one who could hold everything together.

Things were unraveling and my least favorite moment happened when my dad called me into his office to answer some questions.

"What's this I hear about comedians shaking down businesses in the name of the charity golf tournament?" he asked sternly. "I have a report that when a liquor store didn't want to participate in The Comics Open by giving the comedians free beer, those comedians started to picket the liquor store. Five minutes later a fight breaks out between the comedians and the store owner and some of his customers."

I hadn't heard about that one, so I said, "Dad, I'm sure that was just an isolated incident."

My dad cut me off. "That's the problem, Dale. It doesn't appear to be an isolated incident. I'm hearing about cases all over the city where the comedians are using intimidating tactics to get businesses to give things to them in the name of the tournament."

"A few bad apples, Dad, but I'll get on it. I'll have another meeting with all of the comedy clubs and make them start policing themselves."

Dad's questions went from bad to absolutely awful and his eyes seemed to bore a hole in me as he asked coldly, "Have you ever heard anything about drug sales at The Comedy Werks?"

"Absolutely not!" I shot back. "There is no chance of that! I have known the Langley brothers for a long time now and I know for a fact they are anti-drug. And they would never allow anything that could cost them their liquor license and their club." What I told dad was true. What I didn't tell him was that the back parking lot of The Comedy Werks usually smelled like a rock concert.

Dad's expression appeared to mellow a bit and he obviously liked my answer. But what he said next shocked me.

"As a matter of fact their club *is* in jeopardy. If not with us then the guys over at Alcohol Control. And I have received some intelligence that after two in the morning, The Comedy Werks becomes an after-hours club complete with professional dancers from some of the strip clubs around the city."

I didn't have to guess where that information came from and I wanted to say, "There's nothing intelligent about anything Sergeant Harry Herndon would have to say." But instead I offered, "That's an exaggeration at best. Their club is not open to the pubic after closing and no liquor is sold after-hours. If some of the comics brought some strippers in there after-hours then it was for their own amusement."

Dad didn't say anything for a while; he just bored another hole in me with his eyes. He finally spoke, "It was your idea that we support this golf, charity event and I'm on record and on television telling the people of Houston I'm behind The Comics Open. I have political enemies who are watching this tournament closely and they would love to see it become a disaster and see me go down with The Comics Open. It's not you, Dale, but I didn't know your colleagues are such screw-ups. Get them in line!"

I left Dad's office thinking I had to take some sort of drastic action. I felt like I should be Paul Revere, driving through Houston screaming, "The comics are coming!" But I knew if I did that then people would be looking at me strangely and yelling back at me, "We know! They've already been here!"

On the drive from my dad's office to Milt and Marty's office I noticed for the second day in a row, a biplane dragging a sign through the air over Houston that read, "The Comics Open June 17." I drove a little further and then I noticed in the sky at the north end of the city six airplanes had just finished skywriting, "The Comics Open." I wondered aloud, "How did the comics pull that one off?"

I walked into Milt and Marty's office and as I took my seat between their two desks, I pointed in the air and said, "How?"

Milt immediately responded with mock excitement, "The banner being pulled behind the biplane was free! The comics were real proud of that one. But what they didn't understand was that the biplane was that company's contribution to charity, not the skywriting. The skywriting cost us fifteen hundred. We've got the bill to prove it. By the way, we've got lots of bills."

I looked toward Marty who looked just as frustrated as Milt. Marty had a fistful of bills to back up his brother's statement. "That's the new thing," Marty explained to me. "The comics are charging things and having the bills sent to the board of directors of The Comics Open in care of The Comedy Werks."

"That's bad," I said as I shook my head. "That's really bad."

"You want to know how bad?" Milt asked me with a sarcastic smile on his face. "Do you want to know how bad it's gotten? Do you want to know how short we might be on the money? It might go as high as six figures."

"No way! That's impossible!" I said in total disbelief.

"I don't expect you to believe me," Milt said calmly. "But I know you'll believe my source," as he looked at his brother.

I looked at Marty, who was nodding his head. He finally said, "Dale, we might be as much as one hundred thousand short on what we'll owe different charities around the city."

I didn't say anything because I couldn't. When I finally got done shaking my head, I said, "Guys, I hate to play, 'Can You Top This?' with you but I've got worse news."

I snuck a peak at Milt and Marty and even though they looked somewhat interested in what I had to say, their expressions told me that nothing I could tell them could really shock them. I continued, "I just came from my dad's office and he ain't happy. He knows what the comics have been doing and worse than that, he was asking me questions about The Comedy Werks. I know who is feeding him the bullshit information. Even though I smoothed it over with Dad, I think the guy feeding him the bullshit can cause us trouble in the press. Any way you look at it, we're in trouble."

Neither Milt nor Marty seemed too concerned but Milt got to use his favorite expression with me as he said, "Cut to the chase, Chase."

I started to explain. "If The Comics Open ends up being an embarrassment to everyone involved, then my dad is in some political trouble with his enemies. We'll all be in trouble, for that matter. But even if The Comics Open turns out to be a great success, a sergeant in the police department will probably go to the newspapers with the story of how comedians received goods and services in the name of Children's Charities. He is already talking to Alcohol Control about your club."

There was a long pause and then Marty said, "So what you are saying is, there is going to be an earthquake followed by a big fire, but it's okay because after that a giant flood will come along and put out the fire."

"Something like that," I answered.

Marty asked, "Is there any good case scenario in all this?"

"Right now it doesn't look like it," I said. "The bottom line is my dad will be in trouble, which means I will be in trouble." My blood was starting to boil as I said, "I'd give anything if we could take this whole thing back." I went on, "Anyway, your liquor license will probably be revoked long enough to drive you out of business and who knows how that newspaper article will affect the rest of the Houston comedy clubs."

No one spoke for the longest time and then Milt said to no one in particular, "It seemed like such a good idea."

"It was my idea." I said. "And I'm sorry."

"No," said Milt and he was being very philosophical as he continued, "It doesn't matter whose idea it was. It was a good idea. An idea to raise money for Houston charities and in the process raise some goodwill for our comedians and comedy clubs. What's wrong with that? Where did we go wrong?"

Marty said, "It probably seemed like a good idea to open Pandora's box too."

"That was the problem," I said as I looked at Marty. "We opened Pandora's box and let all of the comics loose on the city. They always stayed pretty much at their own clubs until my idea."

"I can control the comedians," said Milt as he laughed sardonically at himself. "The dumbest thing ever said."

No one spoke for a while and as Marty was going through some bills he finally spoke up and said, "Here's a bill we got for a barroom brawl. Who the hell ever got sent a bill for a barroom brawl?"

"I heard about it last night," I said. "But why did you get sent the bill for the damages?"

"It was Clay and his bunch and that queen and her court. Clay had the bar convinced to run their bar tab and then send it over to us in care of the board of directors of The Comics Open. And the bar decided to put all of the damages on the tab too."

"Why not?" said Milt sarcastically. "Why the hell not?"

I thought I might tell the story of the brawl to Milt and Marty for the simple reason the three of us were very depressed and maybe the story might lighten things up a little. That and the fact that we had nothing else to talk about.

"Guys," I started, "an off-duty cop friend of mine I went to high school with—Chris McManus—was in The Rusty Armadillo with his wife having a drink after they had been to a movie. That, as you know from your bill, is where the fight took place. My friend said he didn't use his badge and professional training to break up the fight because it was so damned entertaining, and he had never seen women end up winning a barroom brawl."

Milt and Marty weren't laughing or even smiling but they did look interested enough for me to keep going. "The queen and her court and the guys showed up there and Clay got their bar tab up and running, which started with three bottles of champagne.

"Chris McManus said that the fourteen of them were acting very sophisticated but everyone in the place figured the girls were topless dancers and that's why the trouble started. Apparently there was a table of nine rich-looking young guys who made up a bachelor party. They were fairly drunk and when they saw the girls with the comics, one of the rich guys yelled, 'We were going to go bar hopping at strip clubs but it looks like the strippers have come to us!'

"Billy Meyer immediately jumped up, but Edna 'Too Tall' Jones pulled him back into his chair next to hers and the rest of the girls patted their dates on their backs letting them know they weren't offended. One of the rich guys went over to apologize for his friend but he poured more gasoline on the fire when he added, 'But if you girls want to make some extra money tonight dancing for our bachelor party then just let us know.'"

Milt said, "Oops," and Marty shook his head knowingly. He knew what was coming next.

I went on, "That guy turned and walked back toward his table and when he was halfway there, he was attacked from behind by Billy who rode the guy right into the ground below the bachelor party table. The fight was on. My cop buddy said that the three minority comics fought very well. He, of course, was alluding to Brent Harris, Bobby Sanchez, and Greg Okada. He said one of the smaller comics just stood on his chair and threw things at the rich guys and he had a line for everything he threw."

"Barry Stein!" Milt and Marty yelled out simultaneously.

"Yeah!" I concurred and continued, "Apparently Barry threw an empty champagne bottle at the rich guys as he yelled, 'A Jew throwing a grenade!' He then flung an ashtray at them like a Frisbee as he cried, 'Take that, you Nazi bastards!'"

Milt and Marty laughed for the first time since I started telling the story. I kept going, "Apparently David Luben approached the brawl and with his hands over his head, he yelled, 'Violence is the tool of the ignorant!' He got punched in the mouth shortly after making that statement."

Marty laughed again but Milt only smiled a bit. "Chris described Billy as the toughest. He didn't do much damage but he got up every time he got knocked down and he got knocked down a lot. At one point he decided to get higher ground by standing on the bar. He wanted to swing on a Tiffany lamp over the crowd but he and the lamp came crashing down to the floor as my cop buddy's wife said seriously, 'That will be expensive.'

"At that point Clay got hit to the floor too and that's when the girls decided to take over. Two of the rich guys were stomping on Billy as Edna 'Too Tall' Jones went running in their direction yelling, 'Not my baby you don't!' On a dead run Edna hit one of the guys flush on the side of the head and knocked him down and out. She finished off the second guy in three punches.

"Erla Campbell blindsided the guy her Brent was fighting and that guy went to the floor like a sack of potatoes. Viva Zapata kicked the guy Bobby was fighting and got that guy's attention long enough so Bobby could knock him down. Edna picked up Billy and Jackie helped up Clay. The management finally got in the middle of things and the rich guys didn't want any more to do with the dancers or even the comics. The manager yelled to the queen and her court and the escorts as they were leaving, 'The Comedy Werks will be getting the bill for this!'"

Milt and Marty said simultaneously, "Of course."

I finished up the story. "At that point, Elva Presley turned around and with her best Elvis impression she said, "'Thank you very much.'"

I was laughing a little bit and then Marty said, "Just under two grand. That's what the bill from The Rusty Armadillo was."

"Tiffany lamps are expensive," Milt added nonchalantly.

I just waved as I headed for the door and then Marty stopped me by saying, "Oh yeah, we forgot to tell you. One of the sponsors pulled out. And they took their one thousand dollars with them."

"Which one?" I asked in disgust.

"The video chain," answered Marty. "When they refused to give some comics free movies, those comics acted up in one of their stores. The store's security cameras caught the antics of the comics. They say their newest video is the one they have of those comics pretending to masturbate while looking at the covers of the videos in the adult section. And then they would yell from the adult section of the store to the manager who was waiting on paying customers, 'Hey! Is *Teenage Whip Bitches* a good movie? How about *Surfer Sluts?*'"

I said nothing. My face conveyed to Milt and Marty how totally disgusted I was. Milt finally said optimistically, "Marty and I have an idea to get a couple of guns and start killing comics and when the police start closing in, we turn and shoot each other."

Marty was nodding his head in agreement as I said, "I want to be part of that. Yeah, count me in."

CHAPTER TEN

It was the day before The Comics Open and I snuck in a late breakfast with my parents. I really needed to see them. I needed to share with someone my feeling of impending doom.

My dad counseled me, "Just keep putting out as many fires as possible and stay strong." "Thanks, Dad. I think that's what the mayor of Hiroshima said."

Mom added, "Things always work out for the best."

I smiled at her and responded, "Said the beautiful mother to her son as he was being led off to the firing squad." I decided to tell them the truth. "Dad, I came over to apologize now for what has already happened and for what is probably going to happen tomorrow. I'm sorry I talked you and your department into backing this thing."

My dad said, "The game's not over yet, Dale. You've had some setbacks and it's not looking good, but it's not over yet." He then said something he had told me a thousand times: "Just work hard and stay out of the results."

Mom just kept smiling at me as she repeated herself, "Things always work out for the best."

I heard the song "The Comics Open" on the car radio as I drove to The El Rancho Heights Golf Course and the song lifted my spirits a bit. I kept running my dad's advice over and over in my head. I still had a chance. It wasn't over yet.

It was still before noon when I caught up with Milt, Marty, and the rest of the board of directors in the big meeting room inside the clubhouse of The El Rancho Heights Golf Course. The room held about a hundred people, and there were at least that many organizers and volunteers running in and out of that room all day. It looked like a war room in a military complex the day before a major battle was to take place.

The walls were covered with charts listing names of who and what groups would be in charge of parking, tickets, and refreshments. Who was to be at which tee boxes and what greens. Who the judges were to be for the longest drive competition and the closest-to-the-pin contest. The sponsors who were donating souvenirs, to be sold for the charities at the tournament, as well as which comedy clubs were donating T-shirts and hats. The names of the people who would be selling the merchandise for the sponsors and the comedy clubs were also on the wall. Everything was covered from where the sponsors' signs were to go to first aid, security, and cleanup.

There was excitement in the air and a spring in everyone's step. I overheard one of the teenage volunteers, who was staring at every comedian who went by, tell a girl she was with, "I'm not supposed to talk to any of the comedians. My mother dated a comedian before she met my father and all I know is, I'm not supposed to talk to any of the comedians."

I went over to where Milt and Marty were and asked them, "Anything I can do to help?"

"Dale, can you call your dad and ask him if he can arrest every comedian in town and not let them out until it's time for the show tomorrow night?" Milt asked.

"An APB on all comedians," I said pretending to follow his orders. "That will be a shitload of paddy wagons."

Milt and Marty kept thanking Bobby Ray Sutton. "This is amazing, Bobby," Milt told him. "I knew a lot went into a tournament, but I had no idea how you would organize it and get it all done."

Marty commented to his brother, "I told you we picked the right guy."

"You picked the right guy," Bobby Ray concurred, "because I am the one who knew who would get this done. I knew all of the members of this golf club would get behind it and they knew how to do it. Service groups like to get involved in things like this. We've got the Kiwanis Club helping out, as well as service groups from the high school and the youth group from the First Baptist Church. All of those volunteers bring more volunteers and that's how these golf tournaments get done."

Brenda Brookshire was very involved that day in the meeting room and when Milt tried to thank her for all she was doing, she simply said, "Piece of cake, Milty. This is like organizing my junior prom, senior ball, grad night, and ten-year class reunion all rolled into one—times one million."

Marty was still hard at damage control. He kept a clipboard with him at all times and he asked the comedians to give him the names of every business they made promises to. He also made sure there were signs made up and displayed at the golf course and at the show and announcements made thanking those businesses.

David Luben's father's sign company was working overtime and their contributions were above and beyond the call of duty. David took the opportunity to blackmail Milt and Marty about getting more stage time at their club. "I don't know if we can get all these signs done on time," he told Milt and Marty as he was looking down and shuffling his feet. "And Dad was wondering why I'm working so hard for you guys when you just use me one night a week—on Monday, amateur night. I'm not asking for me, but my dad was kind of wondering."

Milt and Marty immediately saw what David was going for and they gave it to him, for the sake of the tournament. Marty told him, "We have seen some tremendous growth in your stage presence and your comedy writing."

"Yeah," said Milt a little sarcastically, "we were just discussing moving you up to weeknights at our club starting next week. Now, tell me again, do we have any trouble getting these signs on time?"

David excitedly said, "I won't let you guys down. We'll get your signs out on time."

Brenda was finishing up the chart of the players' names and who would be playing with whom and what hole they would be starting from. Brenda spotted Bobby Sanchez first, as he walked into the meeting room carrying a very large cardboard box. Behind him was the dancer Viva Zapata, who was carrying a much smaller box. Bobby and Viva had been almost inseparable since they met Wednesday night.

"Who gets these?" yelled Bobby referring to the boxes.

"Right here," pointed Brenda as Bobby and Viva put their boxes down on a table.

Bobby's box contained the tickets to be sold to the public for the tournament and show. Some tickets had already been sold, but there were about six hundred seats remaining for the show and they were hoping to sell that many tickets for the tournament too. Viva's box contained the official badges and ribbons that would be worn by the players and volunteers and all of the people who didn't have to pay to get in to either event.

Milt and Marty thanked Bobby and Viva, and then Milt asked Bobby whether it was okay for him to talk to Viva for a moment. Bobby replied with a smile, "You don't have to, Milty. I already mentioned it to her."

Viva smiled at Milt, Marty, Brenda, and me as she said, "I know the rules. No flashing of tits tomorrow at the tournament or the show. The other girls know, too."

"Thanks, Viva," said a relieved Milt.

Milt starting calling each comedy club owner and telling them—again—how important the day of the tournament and show was. "Our reputations are on the line tomorrow and more importantly the reputation of Houston comedy in general. The comics have already caused a lot of problems. We might be able to weather the storm if things go well tomorrow." Milt's final comment to each club owner was, "We can either all look good tomorrow or we can all get a black eye or a knockout punch. It's really up to the comics now."

Marty told me, "I have been spending most of my time spreading the word to all the comedy club managers, doormen, bar staff, and most of all, the comics that their actions on Monday could make or break Houston comedy—it's as simple as that. If we screw up on Monday, then the only people we will have screwed is ourselves."

By late afternoon the day before the tournament, the comedians were already out of control. That many comedians getting together for any event had to turn into a big party. The comics from L.A. and New York who wanted to participate had already hit town, and comics from around the country who just wanted to be in town for the party had also arrived. Some crashed at the apartments of the local comics, but most of them had hit a motel called The Starlight, which was across the street from The Sam

Houston Inn, which housed the comics who played The Laff Inn. There were about four comics to a room and things were starting to get ugly at both motels.

The managers of The Starlight Motel were a couple from Pakistan to whom I paid a visit. I immediately saw a little cardboard sign they had put up that read, "We Respectfully Refuse to Be the Official Motel of The Comics Open." They explained that the comedians kept telling them, "You have a chance to be the official motel of The Comics Open. All you have to do is give the comics free rooms." They told me, "We made up that sign after hearing the comics offer that for the fifth time."

I talked to the manager over at The Sam Houston Inn, who told me, "The comics tried to run that be-the-official-hotel-of-The-Comics-Open thing on me but I told them we don't even like the public to know that The Laff Inn comedians stay here. I guarantee you none of them got a room here without putting up a credit card as security."

As I stood in the lobby of The Sam Houston Inn I looked out at the pool. It looked like a scene out of a cheap spring break movie. Instead of college boys there were a lot of comedians around the pool, with a few wannabes and other hangers-on. The women around the pool weren't college coeds, but some comediennes, a few girlfriends, a couple of hookers, and a lot of groupies. They all appeared to be having a lot of fun, but there were two things there that bothered me, and one of them was Packy Hester.

Packy Hester was a five-foot-eight-inch, one-hundred-forty-pound walking drugstore. His eyes were green and red and they always appeared to be bugging out of their sockets. His shoulder-length hair was brown and, like the rest of him, always greasy. His teeth were a pale yellow. Although the cops had suspected him of holding drugs, they never wanted to search him because that would entail having to touch him.

What I knew of Packy Hester I had overheard from the comedians. They said he knew more about drugs than a pharmacist and he bragged of having a fictitious degree in something called chemical engineering. He had gained that knowledge from his extensive reading on the subject of drugs and his own experimentation. One good thing I'll say about Packy is that he wouldn't sell anything he hadn't already tried himself.

Other than sharing pot in the parking lot of The Comedy Werks that one time, drugs were where I drew the line. And I'll admit it, I didn't like Packy Hester. The other thing I'll admit is that Packy was smart. He was hard to notice. He never appeared the same way twice. He would show up in Houston with his hair at his shoulders and I wouldn't recognize him the next night because his hair would be up under his cowboy hat. The next time he would show up with short hair and the next he would be wearing a baseball hat and then the next day he would be gone again.

As I stood in the lobby watching the goings on at the pool, I realized I wasn't the only person who was observing Packy Hester. There was a middle-aged man there who looked completely out of place. He was wearing sunglasses, a Hawaiian shirt with matching shorts, brown socks, and sandals. Sergeant Harry Herndon was about as inconspicuous as a fire hydrant, but no one seemed to notice him because they were having too much fun.

I could tell Sergeant Herndon was enjoying his role as an undercover cop. He was busy taking notes about the comics' drinking beer and smoking marijuana around the pool with some girls who looked under eighteen and some women who were known prostitutes. I watched Herndon's excitement grow as he slowly realized what Packy Hester was doing.

Harry knew why the comics took girls to their rooms and then came out some time later with big smiles on their faces. But he couldn't at first figure out why some of the people around the pool almost seemed to fight over who got to take the skinny little greasy guy to their room next. Harry watched and overheard some things, until he started getting as excited about the character they called "Packy" as he got over some of the girls sitting poolside in their bikinis. It became clear to Harry that Packy was a drug dealer.

I suddenly heard screams from across the street at The Starlight Motel pool and I was just about stampeded by all of the people who were rushing from The Sam Houston Inn pool to investigate the screams. I ducked out of the way so I wouldn't be noticed by Harry Herndon, who was following the crowd.

I slowly followed them all across the street and finally saw what all of the screaming was about. A conga line had started and all of the men who were in it were naked and all the women in that line were topless. Some calypso music was pounding through a makeshift sound system and there were about fifty people in the conga line as they danced around the pool.

I noticed that Sergeant Herndon never took his eyes off that conga line as he wrote in his note pad. He was probably writing "indecent exposure" as he tried to count how many people were in the conga line. He probably never knew how many guys were in that line, but he definitely noticed how many topless women there were.

Sergeant Herndon left The Sam Houston Inn when Packy did and followed Packy, as I followed the both of them. Packy drove first to The Laff A Lot Comedy Club and then downtown to Jokesters. It was only six o'clock, two hours before the show would start at either club. Packy didn't stay very long at either place. At Jokesters he went back out to his car and then back in, although he didn't seem to be carrying anything with him. I could just feel Harry Herndon getting more excited about Packy by the minute.

What Packy was doing was making the rounds to the comedy clubs before their shows started to see if the comics, the doormen, or bar personnel wanted any of his products. He was also informing them of what time he would be back later that night. Harry followed him to The Comedy Werks and watched, from across the street, as Packy went inside. When he came out he was followed by Jimmy Clark, who was as excited to see Packy as a little kid was to see Santa Claus. Packy seemed annoyed by Jimmy and gave him something out of his pocket just to get Jimmy to leave him alone.

Harry Herndon also became interested in Jimmy Clark. Sergeant Herndon wasn't going to go into The Comedy Werks so he took off, but I went inside just to check on things. It turned out that Harry Herndon wasn't the only person interested in Jimmy Clark, because so were Milt and Marty. Jimmy would be performing that night and he was the first one of their comedians they had ever had to cut off from their bar. Brent Harris was one of the bartenders that night and he had strict instructions not to serve Jimmy anything until after his show.

As it turned out, Jimmy could have used a beer or a shot of booze to level himself off. Jimmy had been high on speed ever since Packy had hit town. Jimmy was going onstage that night for fifteen minutes in the second spot.

Milt opened the show by rolling himself onstage to the "Proud Mary" line "Rollin' on the river" and introduced Alex Lewis, who did ten minutes and then took over emceeing the show. Alex introduced Jimmy next and Jimmy almost knocked Alex over as he rushed to the stage.

Because he was high on speed, Jimmy did fifteen minutes worth of material in just under seven minutes. His opening bit was always, "Hi, I'm Jimmy Clark, a good old American boy. I love hot dogs, baseball, big tits, and

apple pie. Just kidding folks, I really don't like apple pie."
He would then go into a rather long routine about how he
felt that it was no coincidence his initials were the same
as Johnny Carson's and Jesus Christ's, and his two biggest goals were to do the Johnny Carson show and then,
when he died, meet Jesus.

The bit almost always worked well and would get him
off to a good start. But that night, because he was high
on speed, the routine sounded like, "Hi! I'm Johnny Carson
and I love America, big tits and initials! My initials are
the same as mine and his and some day I want to do the
Johnny Carson show but if I die on that show then I
won't get into heaven! Jesus Christ, how about those
Houston Rockets!"

Milt took a moment to stare at Brent, who was standing behind the bar across from Alex, who was staring at
the stage in disbelief. Jimmy usually talked about movies
in his act and he had two good bits about two big block-
buster movies, *Ghandi* and *E.T.* Jimmy was talking so
fast he merged those two bits into one Milt described as
"Ghandi meets E.T." The bit sounded like E.T. wanted to
call home and Ghandi wanted him to call for a pizza
because he wanted to break his fast. When Jimmy rushed
from the stage, Alex ran back up to the microphone and
said, "Let's hear it for him, folks! Jimmy Clark! A graduate from the Evelyn Wood Speed Reading School of
Comedy!"

I was across the show room from Milt and we just
shook our heads at each other before I finally waved and
headed out the door. I thought I would make the rounds
to all of the comedy clubs and then, hopefully, get some
sleep so I would be ready for the big day. I figured the
chances of my getting any sleep that night were about the
same as Jimmy Clark getting any and that didn't look
possible.

I quickly found out how crazy Comics Open fever was getting as I turned onto the street The Laff Inn was on and I was stopped by a parade. Coming up the street on both sides were about fifty comedians and at least that many other crazies, about twenty of whom were carrying the twenty-foot by five-foot Comics Open banner that had been displayed at the Astrodome. About twelve people were beating drums and playing other instruments as they tried to simulate a marching band. It was a giant mess, and I could hear sirens in the distance coming to break the whole thing up.

The night before the tournament took on kind of a New Year's Eve atmosphere at all of the comedy clubs. The comics and comedy club personnel were in a party mood, and the audiences quickly got into it. There were so many comics in town, going onstage at all of the comedy clubs, that the shows became extra special and the comics had fun "improv-ing" together and heckling their fellow comics onstage.

One of the comics standing in the back of the show room would yell to the comic onstage, "Hey, Stan! Do you have any naked pictures of your sister?"

"Of course not!" Stan would snap back.

"You want to buy some?" the comic would yell back to Stan.

One of the comics would pretend to help the comic onstage by implying there was trouble with the sound system. "Hey, Dave! You're standing too close to the microphone!"

The comic onstage would then take a half step back and ask, "How's that?"

The comic in the back would yell, "No, back a little further!"

The comic onstage would then take another step back and ask again and then be told once again, "No, back further!"

The comic onstage would finally ask, "How far back do you want me to go?"

"Do you have a car?" all of the comics in the back would answer, as well as some of the audience members who knew the routine.

Some of those lines were as old as vaudeville, but it always amazed the comedians how well those jokes worked with the audiences. A comic in the back would yell to the comic onstage after the comic got a big laugh, "Oh, that's an old joke! What was that, one of your father's jokes?"

The comic onstage would answer back, "What are you, one of your mother's jokes?"

At another club that night, one of the comics in the back of the room yelled to the comic onstage, "Why don't you have a bulge in the front of your pants, like the other comedians?"

After a big laugh, the comic onstage would say, "Hey, I didn't come here to be insulted."

"Where do you usually go?" the comics in the back would yell, as well as some of the audience members.

It was a good night for comedy in all of the comedy clubs in Houston. Closing time meant that most of the comics and their friends would go to The Comedy Werks for the after-hours bar and hijinks in the show room. It was the most people Milt and Marty had ever had after hours, but they didn't mind. They were glad almost all of the comics were there. They wanted to remind them one last time that the fate of comedy in Houston might come down to how they all acted the following day at the tournament and show.

When I got to The Comedy Werks, its show room was filled with more than a hundred comics, plus their friends and groupies. It sounded like New Year's Eve, just after midnight, but it was actually a little after two A.M. They put on the "Proud Mary" theme "Rollin' on the river" to get everybody's attention as Milt rolled to the stage. Everyone laughed at first, but then surprisingly quieted down to hear Milt speak—everyone except Jimmy Clark, who was still high on speed and had been talking nonstop since his set over six hours earlier. Big Bill Blevens took a few steps toward him and Jimmy immediately quit jabbering. He didn't want Bill to put him in a combination headlock and sleeper hold like he did at the press conference.

To Milt, the scene was not unlike any Monday late afternoon when they were organizing the amateurs to go on The open-mike night. Milt got a big laugh when he told the assembled comedians and their friends, "Okay, I want all you amateurs to sign that sheet, because you'll be going onstage for five minutes each later on this evening."

After the laugh, he said seriously, "I've got just two things to say. One, welcome. There are actually some comedians here I haven't met and I want to meet you all. Two, and for the last time, our actions at the tournament and show can make or break comedy in Houston. We're already in a lot of trouble because some of you got free stuff by promising businesses they were the official sponsors of our tournament. They expect some things in return and there are too many of them to make them all happy. Women and even underage girls have been promised things."

Everyone started to giggle or laugh and Milt said, "Yeah, it's funny. It's also illegal and unethical and it will hurt all of our businesses. And the trickledown theory is that if the comedy club owners are hurt, that means less stage time and money for the comedians."

The room quieted down again and Milt continued. "We came up with this idea so we could have some fun, raise some money for charities in the process, and promote goodwill, as well as ourselves. Let's look good at the tournament and show. Thanks."

Everyone started cheering and Marcus Pauley yelled, "Alright, coach! Let's kill 'em! Win one for Milty!" Everyone in the room picked up the chant and "win one for Milty" became the battle cry for the tournament.

Milt was rolling his chair around the room shaking hands with friends and meeting new people. Marty said, "He looks like a politician."

The only person getting around that room more than Milt was Packy Hester. I only noticed him because Jimmy Clark was following him around like a puppy dog. I really didn't pay much attention to Packy because there was so much going on in the show room.

At one point I looked out the front door of The Comedy Werks and Sergeant Harry Herndon was right where I expected him to be. He was sitting in his car across the street, drinking coffee, and he appeared to be going over his notes.

There was a lot of drinking and dancing in the show room and an attempted wheelchair race between Milt's friend Art Harold and one of the comics, but there wasn't really enough room for it. Milt got to meet an L.A. comic by the name of Bruce Robertson, who was performing at The Laff Inn that week. Bruce was a friend of Mark Silverman, the comic who showed up at the press conference and basically promised the people of Houston that Jerry Lewis, Buddy Hackett, Gabe Kaplan, Robin Williams, and other major stars would be showing up the tournament and show. "Do you have that prick's phone number?" Milt asked Bruce.

"Yeah," said Bruce laughingly. "If he's not there you can leave a message on his machine." Milt left the following message: "Mark, this is Milt Langley. I own The Comedy Werks with my brother Marty, and we are currently in the show room where we had the press conference where you promised that all those stars were going to show up for our tournament and show." Milt went from talking very softly to slowly going berserk as he said into the phone, "We were just wondering, where the fuck is Jerry Lewis? And Buddy Hackett! Robin Williams must have gotten lost, because he hasn't shown up either! All of Houston is waiting for them, thanks to you! Can't wait till you play The Laff Inn again you phony, Hollywood, name-dropping prick!"

For the next hour comics kept calling his number and leaving messages of bad impressions of celebrities and stars. I left an impression of Archie Bunker saying, "Hey, Meathead. You shouldn't make promises you can't keep. Isn't that right, Edith?" I then did Edith Bunker saying, "Mark, you're a lying name-dropping phony bastard."

The other comedians left impressions of celebrities that were so bad they didn't even have the voice patterns down, but it really didn't matter. Harry Bosco said into the phone in his attempt at Jimmy Stewart, "Hey, Mark, I'm down here in Houston for The Comics Open with my rabbit Harvey. Where the fuck are you?"

Marcella Mississippi didn't even try. She just said in her own voice, "Hi, this is Redd Foxx. Why didn't you say I was coming to the tournament? Was it because I'm black, you honky, cracker, motherfucker?"

Bobby Sanchez walked into the show room with Viva Zapata, who was wearing hot pants, a Comedy Werks T-shirt, and a sombrero. They were followed by Clay and Jackie "The Golden Bear" Nicklaus and the rest of her court, as well as their escorts, Greg, Barry, David Stein, and Billy Meyer. Billy introduced Edna "Too Tall" Jones to his partner Bill, and Bill said, "Edna, it's so nice to meet you. So you are the reason that young Billy has been acting so human this past week."

Clay took the stage and introduced the queen and her court and everyone applauded wildly, even though none of the girls exposed her tits. There was more drinking and dancing and another conga line, which went on until about three-thirty in the morning. That's when almost everybody left The Comedy Werks. Some weren't leaving to get some sleep for their big day, however; somebody said something about going to play golf.

There were a few comics who were still a little upset about not being allowed to play in the tournament. The alcohol helped them get really mad about it early that morning. "We'll have our own tournament," they murmured amongst themselves.

I watched Harry Herndon as he observed everyone leaving The Comedy Werks at close to four that morning. He probably figured he would go home and get some sleep, just like the comics were probably going to do. Alex Lewis then whispered loudly, "Follow me, I know how to get to the golf course." I knew Sergeant Herndon heard what I heard and he probably didn't think anything of it either. He probably thought like I did that some of the comics were going to sleep in their cars at the golf course and just wake up there, ready to go.

Then Jimmy Clark yelled, "Packy! I know the way to the golf course! I'll ride with you and show ya!"

I wasn't going to follow them but I was sure Herndon was. I figured the first thing that he probably wrote on his note pad was "trespassing," as the comics let themselves through the gate and onto the golf course.

I needed some sleep and I went home to get myself a few hours' worth. I lay down on my couch, but I couldn't keep my eyes shut and I couldn't keep the visions and the voices out of my head. I kept hearing, "We'll still owe about a hundred thousand no matter what happens." I kept seeing newspaper headlines that said "Comedians Rip Off City in Name of Children's Charities." And, "Nothing Funny at Comics Golf Tournament as Twenty-Seven People Are Hurt."

I kept seeing and hearing television reporters saying, "The disaster known as The Comics Open was apparently the brainchild of the son of the chief of police." And, "An unnamed city councilman has said Chief of Police Bertram Chase's job is in jeopardy for being a part of The Comics Open."

When I woke up it was still dark out. My first thought was, "It wasn't even dawn on the day of the tournament and already The Comics Open was off to a horrible start."

CHAPTER ELEVEN

The sun was coming up when I arrived at the golf course. Four Hispanic groundskeepers got there just seconds before I did. The five of us were surprised to find the main gate open and even more surprised to find a 1972 Oldsmobile in the right front sand trap on the eighteenth green, which was right in front of the clubhouse. There were two sets of legs sticking out of the front passenger side window and two sets of legs sticking out the back window. And a guy and a girl were wrapped up in a blanket sleeping on the practice putting green.

I noticed another car over by the ninth green, where there was one comic who sunk a put, as his date applauded from the hood of the car. One of the groundskeepers tapped on the hood of the first car until he awoke two of the five occupants. *"Cuidado,"* said the groundskeeper in Spanish, as he motioned a path for him to drive out of the sand trap. *"Cuidado* means caution," said one of the girls who had been sleeping in the back seat. "He wants you to be careful driving out of here."

The beautifully quiet dawn was broken by the sound of the Oldsmobile starting up, which stirred Harry Herndon, who was sleeping in his car by a chain-link fence in front of the golf course. He couldn't see me but I could see him. He rubbed his eyes and saw the car driving out of the sand trap. The driver of the car on number nine responded to the waves of the groundskeepers by starting his car (along with the comic who was putting with his date on the hood of the car) and driving toward the gate where they had entered.

I told the comics, "You only did one thing smart and that was you didn't drive your cars onto any of the greens. Damage to the greens could have brought an end to the tournament before it ever started and would have driven the tab completely out of sight."

The couple sleeping on the practice putting green hadn't done any damage. I looked around, but I couldn't find any more comedians or problems.

I was looking at Harry Herndon as he reached for his note pad when we both heard the roar of a car engine. I looked in the direction of the far corner of the golf course, as did the four groundskeepers.

In just moments, we all saw coming around the ninth tee box and then up the eighteenth fairway, a car that had no muffler. Alex Lewis's late 1960s Ford had lost its muffler when they tried to jump the cart path between the seventh and thirteenth tee boxes. If the sound of the Oldsmobile starting up had broken the quiet of the early dawn, then Alex's mufflerless car, in comparison, sounded like the world was coming to an end.

Three winos started running out of some bushes where they had been sleeping. The birds were in a panic, as well as tree and ground squirrels. Alex Lewis wasn't driving his car because he was skiing behind it, pulled by a rope tied to the rear bumper. He was naked except for his jockey shorts, ski goggles, ski boots, and snow skis and poles. Steven Reed was driving the car and sitting next to him was his girlfriend, and next to her, Packy Hester.

Jimmy was screaming out of the rear window and Alex's girlfriend was riding on the hood of the car.

The groundskeepers waved at the car to slow down and it abruptly stopped. Alex skied into the trunk of his car as his girlfriend flew off into the waiting arms of one of the groundskeepers. Harry Herndon couldn't really believe what he had just seen and he had no idea what to write down on his note pad. I had no idea what to say to those in the car so I just pointed to the street.

Steven Reed parked the Ford across the street and they all left in Packy's car. Harry Herndon probably figured it would be a good time to go home and get cleaned up and then come back to observe the tournament. I'm sure he heard a call over his police radio instructing the closest patrolman to check out a loud disturbance at The El Rancho Heights Golf Course, a "possible car without a muffler." I'm also just as sure Harry didn't respond. He probably just headed home.

The tournament was to start at ten that morning. Eighteen foursomes would go to each tee box and tee off all at once when they heard the blank fired from a starter pistol. Some of the members of the course got in nine holes before that ever happened and the secretary of The El Rancho Heights Golf Course handled many phone calls from local residents inquiring about the tremendous roar that was coming from the course at dawn.

All of the volunteers and officials were at the golf course by eight that morning, which was also when Milt and Marty arrived. They asked me how things were going and I didn't bother them with what had gone on earlier.

All the signs and banners were up around the course to signify who was sponsoring each tee box. The refreshment and souvenir stands around the course were stocked and manned. The comics were starting to trickle in and weatherwise it was shaping up to be a beautiful day.

There was the sound of balls being hit on the driving range and the usual chatter around the practice putting green and clubhouse. A makeshift sound system that could be heard around the clubhouse area and first tee and eighteenth green was being tested. One of the comics took the microphone from the man who was testing it and said into the microphone, "Testing, testicles one, two, testicles one, two." The man who was originally testing it wrestled the microphone away from the comic.

Another rumbling was heard and then another sound system. Jake Davis was driving his big rig up the street in front of the golf course and honking his horn and yelling into a microphone and speaker he had in his truck, "Jake Davis! The Trucker Comic welcomes y'all to The Comics Open! Have a lot of laughs and spend a lot of money, because it's all for charities. And I just want to say Hi! From Red Haskins and his Texaco Truck Stop out there on 59. Red Haskins' Texaco Truck Stop is the official truck stop of The Comics Open!"

There were already cars parked on either side of the street and no way to get around Jake and his truck (that had no business being in a residential area in the first place). And neither did the other big rig that came down the street heading right for Jake's truck before it stopped. There was also a big banner on the side of its trailer and it was also advertising a sponsor. The only difference was the sponsor that truck was promoting was Jesus Christ.

The Truckers for Jesus had heard Jake advertising The Open over his CB radio, so the Truckers for Jesus truck thought that it would be a nice event to spread the word. Randall Liscombe was a trucker who had accepted Jesus into his life five years earlier when he was trying to kick speed, alcohol, and what Jake described as "a penchant for wearing women's panties." Randall turned his engine off right in front of Jake, and said into his own microphone and out of his own speaker, "Truckers for

Jesus also want to welcome you here today! We want you to give your money to the charities and your lives to Jesus! That can all happen right here today!"

Jake said into his microphone, "Randall, this ain't your deal so you back that truck up about twenty miles and get the hell out of here!"

Randall said into his microphone, "That's right! It's not my deal; it's the Lord's deal! And Jake, I want you to stop backing up and step forward and speaking of hell, that's where you're headed!"

Most of the people who had been on the driving range and putting green and everyone else who was around the clubhouse watched as Jake jumped from the hood of his truck onto the hood of the Truckers for Jesus truck. Randall Liscombe was screaming into his microphone, "You can't stop the word of the Lord, Jake Davis!" He then started quoting scripture as Jake started wrestling with the speaker that was in the grill of Randall's truck.

When Jake failed to remove and destroy the speaker he headed for the cab of the truck and started kicking the door and then the windshield. That brought out the other trucker in the cab who did not seem to be as spiritual as Randall because instead of a Bible, he was carrying a tire iron. That development brought out all of the comics who had been watching the incident because, bottom line, Jake was a fellow comic and he appeared to be in big trouble.

I ran from the first tee box area through the club-house and out of the front door where I passed Marty who was running as he pushed Milt in his wheelchair. We heard Randall screaming scriptures—part of the story of David and Goliath—and, "Lord, please help Jake Davis accept the beating that is about to be laid upon him."

Meanwhile, Jake was bleeding from the head and Randall's partner was standing on the hood of the truck holding off the rest of the comics. The man with the tire iron looked like Davey Crockett during his last moments defending the Alamo. Then he slipped and fell down to the pavement where Jake commenced to put a terrible beating on the man.

Some of the comics were kicking the man Jake was beating until Milt, Marty, and I made them all stop. The teenagers from the El Rancho Baptist Church watched as Jake tried to tear the banner off Randall Liscombe's truck, until I talked him out of it. So Jake just wiped his bloody scalp on it. Randall's friend was put back into the cab and Randall's last words into his microphone were, "I will leave and go away and return to preach another day!" Randall was mooned by four of the comics who Milt and Marty quickly told to pull their pants back up.

Jake moved his truck over to the school parking lot where the show was to be held and Marcus Pauley rode with him. Everybody else started back down the street to the entrance of the golf course where they were confronted by a white church school bus with the words "Inner-City Baptist Church" written on the sides of it. Behind it were two more traditional yellow school buses filled with black children.

The Reverend Luke Witherspoon stepped from the bus carrying a Bible. He immediately recognized Milt and Marty from the televised press conference. The reverend's first words were directed right at the brothers: "These are the children from the ghettos and the projects. Your tournament promised them one thousand dollars each and I'm here to make sure the children get the money they were promised."

Milt ordered everyone to go back to the golf course as Marty started the negotiations with Reverend Witherspoon. I immediately recognized the reverend who had been on the news many times taking up the plight of the poor and the children. He was good at spreading guilt and shaking down businesses and major corporations for donations for his followers. He had a large enough congregation and enough influence to make the word "boycott" strike fear into the hearts and wallets of many Houstonians. He loved to use the televised news as one of his major weapons.

"Welcome," said Marty to the reverend. "I'm glad you're here and I want everybody to have a good time and I want to clear up the mistake that was made at the news conference."

The reverend, too, was cordial but insisted that "something had to be done," and, "the news trucks will be here and they will get pictures of these bus loads of disappointed children."

Marty explained they could afford one dollar a kid but one thousand was insane. Reverend Witherspoon said, "One dollar is a start." He said in a low voice to Marty, "But somebody is going to get a thousand dollars."

So that was it. Reverend Witherspoon would get one thousand dollars under the table and he would speak at the show and to the news cameras about what a great job The Comics Open did for the children. The children in the buses would get free sodas, hot dogs, and passes to the show. The children were let out of the buses and they started running through the golf course like it was a park.

Most of the comics and comedy club personnel had arrived, and if they were there, that meant Packy Hester was also there. He arrived in his car followed, not too closely, by Sergeant Harry Herndon, who obviously had not been home to sleep or to clean up. He was still wearing the yellow Hawaiian shirt with the matching shorts and brown socks and sandals. Harry didn't look too good, but he looked great compared to Jimmy Clark who was walking around in a daze complaining that no one would buy him a beer.

Harry Herndon put on some sunglasses and bought a program and stuck his note pad inside of it. I saw him write something on his note pad, which I assumed was "child endangerment," as he observed some of the inner-city kids playing out on the driving range.

The meeting room in the clubhouse was filling up with the people who were actually going to play in the tournament. There were members of the corporations and businesses that were sponsoring the tournament. There were four DJs from two of the radio stations and even Lance Childress, the cohost of the television show, *Good Morning, Houston.*

Then there were the comedians who walked in wearing brand new golf outfits they had acquired from stores around the city. They all seemed to be wearing some kind of hat, from good-looking golf visors and baseball style hats, to the ridiculous, such as cowboy hats, berets, and a pit helmet. There was also a comic wearing a Hawaiian-style straw hat and another was wearing an English Sherlock Holmes–looking hat. Burt Surgess, the house emcee at Hilarities, was wearing a Houston Astros batting helmet, and Bob Gloster, the manager of Hilarites, was wearing an Oilers football helmet. Both claimed their helmets were for protection, since they had recently undergone brain surgery and now had plates in their heads.

When the comics and other players entered that meeting room, they walked under a banner that read, "Our Goal for the Charities—$250,000!!!" I took Brenda Brookshire aside and as I pointed to that sign I said, "From what I hear, that's how much we might lose."

Brenda said flatly, "Dale, we're in a lot of trouble. I hope people think it was all a joke, since comedians did this, because we're barely halfway there on the money the charities have been promised. Who knows what the repercussions could be from this, but they could be disastrous. Our four big sponsors donated fifteen thousand each and we have six others who put in five grand apiece. We've got a lot of smaller businesses that have given what they can. Money keeps trickling in from around the city and there is still the money from the tournament and tonight's show."

Brenda got very serious for a moment as she said, "Dale, I don't know if Marty has told you or not but we might be as high as six figures short on this thing."

Milt yelled at me and waved me over and had me sit in a chair next to his wheelchair. Milt said, "Dale, as you know, we're in a lot of trouble and I got an idea and I'm going to need your help."

"Sure, Milt," I said. "What do you need?"

"I figure," said Milt, "that this tournament and the show later on could provide a good diversion and alibi for when one of us on the board commits a major crime, armed robbery like a bank or something. You grew up in a cop family—I need your input on this, Dale."

"I think the diversion should be the mass murder of the comedians," I said seriously.

Milt laughed and said, "Dale, the only favor I want is when they send the police to arrest me and my brother, you call ahead to your dad and get us a nice jail cell."

All I said was, "I'll try to get you the cell next to mine."

That meeting room was filled to the brim with comics and one-liners, questions and answers. Frank Lowry was wearing a black visor, black golf shirt, and black golf pants. Harry Bosco yelled across the room, "Hey, Frank! Nice outfit! I didn't know Johnny Cash was making a line of golf clothes!"

"Who sponsored you?" Frank Lowry yelled back. "The Salvation Army?"

"Hey, Bill!" a comic yelled to Bill Blevens. "Where's your partner?"

"With Edna 'Too Tall' Jones!" Bill yelled back.

"Billy only comes up to Edna's tits!" yelled the comic.

"That's why he's with her," answered Bill.

"Hey, Mike! Where did you get that silly-looking shirt?"

"At your sister's apartment!" answered Mike. "I woke up there this morning and she had all sorts of men's clothing in her closet and she told me to pick something out. I almost picked a purple suit with a matching wide-brimmed hat!"

"Where's Ronny?"

"He's not done throwing up yet!" came an answer.

"I'm not proud of this, but I watched Jerry Walters get dressed this morning. His jock strap didn't fit, so he put it on backwards!"

"Hey, Paul! How'd you come out on that sodomy with a sheep charge?"

Paul answered, "I got a good lawyer and he got the charge reduced to 'just following too close.'"

"Does your handicap double if you haven't been to bed yet?"

A comic who had flown in from L.A. the night before yelled to a friend across the room, "That friggin' airline still hasn't found my bags!"

His friend yelled back, "That's what you get for flying Amelia Earhart Airlines!"

Bobby Ray Sutton entered the room and all of the women gasped at how good he looked. He was wearing a perfectly tailored golf outfit in white with pink trim and a white visor and matching shoes. Bob Wurley, the representative from the sportswear company, said to no one in particular, "Bobby Ray is prettier than my wife."

Bobby Ray looked too perfect and the comics weren't about to let him get away with it, without at least a little ribbing. "Hey, Bobby Ray! You look like the illegitimate son of Mr. Clean and the Avon lady!"

Someone yelled, "He looks like the cover boy for *Gay Golfer* magazine!"

Bobby Ray just laughed and walked over to a podium to welcome everyone and get the names of some of the out-of-town comics whom he had never met. He then introduced the sponsors who would be playing. At that point Clay and Queen Jackie walked in complete with her court and their escorts. Jackie and the girls were wearing hot pants, sneakers, and tight Comedy Werks T-shirts.

One of the comics yelled, "Show us your tits!" and there was snickering. The girls had become more like girlfriends to Bobby Sanchez, Brent Harris, Greg Okada, Barry Stein, and David Luben. Billy Meyer yelled, "Who said that?"

A voice yelled back, "I did! Why? What are you going to do about it?"

Billy ran in the direction of the voice, as about twelve comics grabbed him and his partner Bill grabbed the comic who had yelled out. Bobby Ray yelled from the podium, "That's the kind of camaraderie we want to display out there today!"

Things settled down and everyone got to meet the members of their foursome. They also found out to which tee box they were to report. Marty spoke next. "This is our first tournament and we didn't do everything right. Some of the sponsors are rightfully mad because they didn't get the exclusives they wanted. Others gave up some things and they are going to get almost nothing in return."

It was the most serious I had ever heard Marty speak and it was obviously having an impact on the comics, because they were actually listening. Marty continued. "It also appears we're going to fall way short of the money that's already been promised to certain charities. It doesn't look good and most of it is out of our control now. But let's concentrate on what we can control, which is seeing how nice we can be to the public today, and how great a show we can do tonight. What do you say?"

There was a short pause and then Marcus Pauley who had just walked in with Jake Davis yelled, "Let's win one for Milty!" And everyone else picked up the cheer.

The seventy-two golfers and assorted officials and volunteers walked out of that room like a team going to battle. Then the man on the public address system said, "Let's hear it for our players!" and a nice round of applause went up from the crowd of over a thousand people.

Out of nowhere the biplane dragging "The Comics Open" sign made a low pass over the golf course, which added to the excitement. I fully expected the planes that did the skywriting to do a flyby but apparently fifteen hundred dollars didn't include buzzing a golf course.

Linda Hart was there as well as Larry Lawrence with twelve members of The Gay Men's Chorus of Houston. Linda led them in singing "God Bless America." It was a nice rendition, but not everyone appreciated the chorus' tight-fitting white tank tops and pink hot pants. Queen Jackie and her court acted like cheerleaders and jumped up and down after the anthem was sung. Many of the men and boys loved the way the queen and her court's breasts bounced up and down when they jiggled with enthusiasm.

Charlie "Chuck" Cutter was manning the PA system and he was drunk by nine forty-five that morning. He was a former country western singer turned radio disc jockey. He was very funny and he performed at celebrity golf tournaments all over the south. Charlie Chuck was in his seventies and kind of a celebrity around Houston.

Charlie Chuck welcomed everyone at the beginning of the tournament and then asked for another round of applause for "those pretty boys in the pink panties who sang." He then pointed to Jackie "The Golden Bear" Nicklaus and said, "That girl right there could breast feed this entire tournament!" Milt about jumped out of his chair and Marty told Clay to get ready to take over the announcing. The board of directors didn't know who invited him, but the four of them fired him and had him hauled away after his comments about the foursome on the first tee box. Bobby Ray was looking around to see people's reactions and the air was filled with nervous giggles.

At exactly ten that morning, I was given the honor of declaring the tournament open. I imagine everyone figured I got the honor because my dad was the chief. But Milt gave it to me because, as he said, "This whole thing was Dale's idea anyway." I told Milt I would do it if he promised not to tell anymore people that it was my idea. I was introduced and I took the microphone and said, "On behalf of the chief of the Houston Police Department, I declare The Comics Open golf tournament open!" I then nodded to the policeman who was standing next to me and he fired a blank from his service revolver into the air as Charlie Chuck yelled into the sound system, "There's the shot signifying the official start of The Comics Open! That was either a gunshot or one of my brothers is here today and apparently he had chili for breakfast!"

The volunteers were trying to clear the inner-city kids off the fairways and tee boxes so the golfers could tee off. In the foursome on the first tee were Carl Stevens, the representative from a sporting goods company, and a DJ by the name of Rockin' Robby. Brenda Brookshire was playing, as well as Dave Galvin, the bar manager of Jokesters Comedy Club.

Charlie Chuck was pretty good at introducing and getting a nice round of applause for the four players on the first tee box, but it was his comments after each one of them teed off that got him removed. Rockin' Robby sliced his tee shot right into some tree branches and it fell straight down onto a teenager's head. Charlie Chuck said, "The only thing uglier than Rockin' Robby's swing is the girl I saw him with last night."

Many people around the first tee box were surprised by that comment and appalled by his next one. The sixty-year-old Carl Stevens teed off and hit one straight, but not too far, which caused Charlie Chuck to comment, "He swings the club like an old man screws. He doesn't take it back very far and he doesn't follow through like he used to."

Marty and Bobby Ray were moving Clay into position to take over for Charlie Chuck, when Dave Galvin hit a wild tee shot deep and down the left-hand side. "There's somethin'!" yelled Charlie Chuck. Then, "Old Dave's swing is like masturbation. It brings him some pleasure, but it is disgusting for other people to watch."

Marty and Bobby Ray sat Clay down next to Charlie Chuck and they told him Clay would take over while they talked to him. Charlie Chuck was arguing with them, but he was picked up, chair and all, after one of the inner-city kids approached him and Charlie Chuck said into the microphone, "Get that pickaninny away from me!"

Brenda was relieved that Charlie Chuck was removed before he had a chance to make any embarrassing statements about her. She told me, "If that old man would have embarrassed me then the next sound he would have heard would have been my driver caving in the side of his head."

Some of the crowd started to disperse and head out to all corners of the golf course. A lot of the men and boys started to follow Queen Jackie and her court around. The girls enjoyed the attention as they signed autographs and took pictures with as many men who asked.

Many of the crowd stayed around the first tee box and were entertained by Linda Hart, Larry Lawrence, and The Gay Men's Chorus as they sang show tunes. The first one they sang was "Oh, What a Beautiful Mornin'" from the musical, *Oklahoma*. My favorite was the second song they sang, which was also from *Oklahoma*. Larry and the twelve men joined arms and swayed as Linda lead them in singing,

"I'm as corny as Kansas in August,

High as a flag on the Fourth of July.

If you'll excuse the expression I use,

I'm in love with a wonderful guy."

Clay announced the next foursome that came to the first tee box, which included Bobby Sanchez, Rick Perry, a newspaper entertainment columnist by the name of Jack Doby, and Robert Wilson, an executive from the supermarket chain sponsor. Clay introduced Bobby Sanchez as "a great comedian and graduate of Pasadena High School. Bobby didn't graduate in the top half of his class but he was quoted as saying that he did feel he helped make the top half possible."

Clay added, "Caddying today for Bobby Sanchez is Viva Zapata, who happens to be a graduate of the Houston Conservatory of Dance." Viva waved to the crowd and winked at Clay.

Rick Perry was introduced by Clay as "a graduate of El Rancho Heights High School!" And, "Rick was voted by his graduating class as Most Likely to Be Incarcerated."

Clay said of the newspaper columnist, "Jack Doby couldn't go to his twenty-year high school class reunion because he wrote a bad check to go to his fifteen-year class reunion. That's how he started his writing career— by writing bad checks."

Clay described Robert Wilson as being from "Lubbock, Texas, where they don't have high schools. The Lubbock school system only goes up to the fifth grade; but Robert did, in fact, graduate from the fifth grade when he was seventeen years old."

I said "Hi" to some old friends and shook hands with some friends of my parents, but my heart wasn't really in it. I was walking on eggshells as my eyes kept darting around looking for trouble.

There were three television news cameras around the first tee. They all got an interview with Milt in his wheelchair and next to him, his "new best friend," a seven-year-old girl in a wheelchair. There were shots of the little girl and other kids being entertained by the comedians and The Gay Men's Chorus. An out-of-town comic was juggling a golf ball, a bowling ball, and a golf club to the delight of the crowd. It was great press and if nothing else, the tournament was looking good on television.

Bobby Ray Sutton was also one of the reporters' favorites and Reverend Witherspoon didn't need any prodding from Marty to get himself interviewed. He talked of "the great work the comedy community of Houston is doing" and he added, "Come on out! There's fun for the entire family!" At that moment Clay yelled into the PA system, "Incoming!" as a golf ball went whizzing by Reverend Witherspoon's left ear.

All of the news reporters signed off by saying, "We'll be out here all day so you can still make it to the golf tournament! Then come to the show tonight at El Rancho Heights High School auditorium, which starts at seven o'clock. We're having a ton of fun and all of the money goes to Children's Charities!"

I figured I would be on the news again, reading the statement from the chief declaring the tournament open.

I just hoped that my posture was good. The last person I wanted to disappoint was my mother.

I started scanning the golf course for trouble and the only real trouble at the moment were the inner-city kids who were running wild through the golf course. I noticed they seemed to be Sergeant Herndon's main interest, because he kept looking in all directions at the kids as he scribbled in his note pad.

Jimmy Clark finally found someone to buy him a beer. It always amazed me how drunks find each other. The last time I saw Charlie Chuck he was incensed to have been relieved of his announcer's job, but now he had his arm over Jimmy Clark's shoulders as they stood in front of the beer tent. I overheard Charlie saying, "You're right Jimmy, we're just not appreciated around here." And, "Give us a couple of more beers over here, bartender."

The next foursome Clay introduced at the first tee included Bobby Ray Sutton who got the largest ovation of the day. The women especially went crazy when Bobby Ray strode to the tee box as Clay simply said, "Ladies and gentlemen, our very own PGA touring pro, the pride of Houston, Bobby Ray Sutton!"

The only thing more exciting than the cheer that went up for Bobby Ray was the drive he hit. I thought he was going to wait because there was a group of inner-city kids standing in the middle of the fairway out about where I thought Bobby Ray would hit the ball. Even one of the members of the golf club, who was an official on the first tee, said, "Better wait, Bobby Ray. They're out there over two and a quarter."

Bobby Ray just teed it up and hit a low screamer that looked like a plane taking off as it slowly gained altitude and screamed down the fairway. It cleared the inner-city kids by twenty feet high and over twenty-five yards long as we saw the ball bounce behind them. The crowd went wild and even I had goose bumps. The comic standing next to me said, "That drive ought to get Bobby Ray laid."

The next person introduced got almost as big an ovation as Bobby Ray did. He was one of the most respected men in Houston and he got a huge hand as Clay said into his microphone, "The head of The Children's Hospital of Houston, Dr. Walter Kellogg!"

Right before Dr. Kellogg teed up his ball, Clay told the crowd, "In Dr. Kellogg's first year out of medical school he accidentally performed an autopsy on a man that was just taking a nap."

Big Bill Blevens was also in that foursome and was introduced by Clay as, "One half of the comedy team of Bill and Billy. Let's hear it for Bill Blevens!"

Clay went on to say about Bill, "Look how big he is, ladies and gentlemen. He was even a big baby. He was born on April fourth, fifth, and sixth. Last summer he worked at the Texas State Fair as a ride!"

Bill crushed his drive and if it had gone straight, it might have gone as far as Bobby Ray's ball. But Bill's ball hooked radically and headed over the fence and toward the street and the next sound we heard was shattering glass.

Clay said into his microphone, "Ladies and gentlemen, on page three in your programs, see the advertisement for Holister's Glass. Specializing in car windshields and windows for your home or business—it's Holister's Glass. Just dial six four seven, eighty five hundred."

Things were going very well and I even let myself relax a little bit. Jimmy Clark and his new friend Charlie "Chuck" Cutter were still happily standing in front of the beer tent. Sergeant Harry Herndon was still wandering around but it appeared he hadn't been able to find any major offenses to write down in his notebook.

I was surprised at what good behavior the comics were displaying, especially around the first tee and clubhouse. Three improvisational players from one of the comedy clubs came dressed as The Marx Brothers. They got to fighting with three improv players from another club who came as The Three Stooges. The crowd was loving it.

The spectators were wondering where the celebrities were so they could get autographs and pictures. They were convinced to settle for the stars of tomorrow. The spectators really didn't have any recourse in the matter, and the comics were very entertaining as they sold the folks on settling on them. "Get autographs and get your pictures taken with these Houston comedians!" one of the comedians yelled. "They will all be stars someday! Beat the crowds and get their autographs now!"

Linda Hart, Larry Lawrence, and The Gay Men's Chorus continued their tribute to Rodgers and Hammerstein as the went from the musical *Oklahoma* to *South Pacific* and sang a medley of songs that included "Some Enchanted Evening" and "I'm Gonna Wash That Man Right Outta My Hair."

Hank Bruno was in the next foursome that came to the first tee and Clay got him a big round of applause by saying, "Let's hear it for the owner of The Comedy Corral Comedy Club, Hank Bruno!"

Hank was loving it. Clay, who knew Hank loved to talk about his years in the Navy, told the crowd, "Hank Bruno had quite a career in the United States Navy. He shot down four airplanes and that's while he was still stateside. He was then shipped to the Philippines, where he served four years in the stockade after being convicted on morals charges."

Although he had to smile, Hank was no longer loving it, and he didn't care for what Clay told the crowd next. "Hank was arrested for selling military secrets to the Russians, but the treason charges were dropped when the specifications for that secret radar system turned out to be the blueprints for an eight-track car stereo."

Also in Hank Bruno's foursome was Houston comic Fred Huggins and Clay told the crowd, "Fred's military service was spent in Canada." Fred thrilled the crowd by hitting an exploding gold ball that had been given to him by Barry Stein.

Clay next introduced in that same foursome, "New York comic and Laff Inn favorite, Tony Gato! Playing with Tony today is his parole officer, Harry Bosco."

Marty pushed Milt up to me and Milt said excitedly, "Dale, things are going great!"

Milt had a big smile on his face and Marty was smiling because his brother was. "Yeah," I said. "Things are going great, so enjoy it. It's about time something went great with this thing."

"Yeah," said Milt. "Let's enjoy the day."

"Be proud, guys," I told Milt and Marty, as I waved my hand around the golf course. "Look at all of the people enjoying themselves and you created all that. I don't know what is going to happen tonight, tomorrow, or even five minutes from now. Let's quit worrying about what might happen and just enjoy this while we can."

It was good advice and I was glad it made Milt and Marty happy. They deserved to get a little joy out of The Comics Open. They had worked hard so they were entitled to something good. I laughed a sick laugh to myself as I said, "Why shouldn't they have a little happiness before they lose everything? Even a man going to the electric chair is given his favorite dinner before he is fried."

My little speech might have sounded good to Milt and Marty, but it sure didn't make me feel better. I figured I wasn't going to be feeling good any time soon. I was walking around with that hole in the pit of my stomach as I cussed the night I had stopped by The Comedy Werks and got my idea for The Comics Open.

Why was I hanging around The Comedy Werks so much? I had fallen into a trap in comedy my father once told me many cops fall into. Some cops spend too much time hanging out with other cops, drinking too much, rehashing what they feel they did to save society from the bad guys. It wasn't a career move to hang out and drink with comedians every night. I was well aware that comedians had far too much time on their hands and alcoholism appeared to be an occupational hazard. The way things were going, I figured I was destined to become an old alcoholic doorman at a comedy club who got to go onstage if no one else showed up. And every once in a while someone would point at me and say, "That's the guy who got the idea for The Comics Open a long time ago. He got the idea that killed comedy in Houston for a lot of years."

The only profanity I heard during the tournament was the usual "Oh, shit!" from the golfer who had missed an easy putt or shanked a shot. That and the profanity I was muttering to myself under my breath. I was feeling sick as I pondered the repercussions of The Comics Open for me, my dad, and comedy in Houston.

The only thing shocking about the golf tournament was the fact that the comics continued to be on such good behavior. Maybe they all had a moment of clarity and figured it was time to do something positive after all the damage they had done. Or maybe they figured it was finally "Show time!" and time for them to perform their magic. Maybe they were looking at the tournament the same way they were looking at the show later that night. It was time to start entertaining and making people happy.

I occasionally checked Jimmy Clark and Charlie "Chuck" Cutter, as well as Sergeant Herndon, and none of them appeared to be causing any problems—at least not for the moment. The inner-city kids were so far out of control that worrying about them wasn't even a worthwhile concept.

When Clay wasn't introducing the next foursome on the first tee, the comedians were making humorous announcements into the microphone. "Attention please! The person who lost the keys to their Mercedes Benz! Thank you for donating your car to The Comics Open and Children's Charities of Houston!"

They made another announcement, which was a standard at all of the comedy clubs. "Attention! The person who had five hundred dollars with a rubber band wrapped around it—we found your rubber band!"

My favorite announcement was one I had never heard before. One of the comics said into the sound system, "Mr. Phil Larkin! We have an important telephone message for you! The Gay Roommate Service called and they said they have found you a roommate!"

A middle-aged man with a big smile walked up to me and asked, "Do you happen to know when Willie Nelson is going to get here?"

I smiled back at him and said, "About the same time the President of the United States is going to show up."

He gave me a strange look and I pointed over to Jake Davis and said, "See that man right there that's built like a fire hydrant? He's Willie Nelson's representative. You go ask him about Willie Nelson."

I started to walk down the side of the first fairway to see how things were going out at the other parts of the golf course and I heard Clay say into the PA system, "How many people have woke up in the morning with Bonnie Praline?" A big roar went up from the crowd and Clay said, "I heard she sleeps around a lot! Ladies and gentlemen, let's hear it for the costar of *Good Morning, Houston*! Bonnie Praline!" The crowd went wild with screams and applause.

Meanwhile, the play on the course was slow for a number of reasons. First of all, few of the players were any good. The ones who could play couldn't concentrate because of all the distractions—that and the fact that there were so many of the inner-city kids on the fairways and greens. The players finally got mad and just started hitting into the kids and the only area that got more business than the beer booths was the first-aid tent.

The longest delay was caused by one of the inner-city kids who figured out that all he had to do to drive a golf cart was to get in and put his foot down on the gas pedal. He drove around aimlessly, yelling to his friends, "All you have to do is put your foot down on the pedal!"

Pretty soon the kids were taking the carts that were left alone by the players who were putting out, going to the bathroom or getting refreshments. In minutes, more than twenty carts were weaving around the course as the participants yelled, and the gallery screamed and hid behind trees or ran out of the way.

The psychic vision of Patty, the waitress, turned out to be true as two golf carts did in fact end up floating in the lake. The people putting out of the fifteenth green pulled the inner-city kids out of the water. None of the kids appeared to know how to swim.

Two of the kids made one of the refreshment stands a drive-through as they plowed into it without stopping. When Reverend Witherspoon saw the kids driving the golf carts, he got three of his assistants to get out on the course and try to control the kids. I figured controlling those kids meant keeping the damage they would do under ten thousand dollars.

I grabbed a golf cart and started driving around the course yelling to the players, "Do not leave your carts unattended! If you get out take the key with you!"

A player who had lost his cart screamed at me, "I don't care about the cart! But get me my golf bag back!"

One of the comics yelled to me, "Stay on it, Dale! You finally get to be a cop!"

Staying busy solving problems on the golf course kept me from worrying about my own problems and that was good. I noticed that Milt and Marty were doing the same thing.

Milt and Marty were touring the golf course talking to the people who had been promised money and business representatives who were upset. They kept telling people, "Just come to the show tonight. You'll have a great time and I guarantee you your business will be mentioned."

Barry Stein was carrying around a giant golf bag and he kept pulling funny props out of it. He also handed out exploding golf balls to the comics, set off a number of smoke bombs around the course, and shot different colored flares into the air. I was standing behind a man who was watching it all and I heard him say to his wife, "You always used to ask me what Vietnam was like. Well, it looked a lot like this."

At about one o'clock that afternoon the rock group Big Shrimpy and The Crabs unexpectedly showed up and, although I couldn't see them, I sure could hear them—and I was at the far end of the golf course. All five of them were there, including an electrical wizard roadie of theirs who got all the guitars hooked up through some outlets in the clubhouse. They had their own amplifiers and, if nothing else, Big Shrimpy and The Crabs were loud.

The crowd gave them a warm welcome when they played their new hit, "The Comics Open." The group didn't interfere with Clay's announcements, and played musical numbers in between foursomes coming to the first tee.

Because Big Shrimpy and The Crabs took over the area by the clubhouse and the first tee, Linda Hart, Larry

Lawrence and The Gay Men's Chorus strolled through the golf course as they sang. The crowd following them seemed to get larger as they went. It was a beautiful moment when Linda, Larry, and the chorus got to an area between the ninth hole and tenth tee box. On a grassy knoll that could be seen throughout the course, the chorus held hands and formed a circle and slowly danced counterclockwise as they sang the song "Getting to Know You" from the musical *The King and I*. Inside the circle, Linda and Larry danced like they were champion ballroom dancers. Many women dabbed their eyes during the number and applauded wildly at its conclusion.

I thought my dad's advice to me was just a metaphor, "Put out as many fires as possible and stay strong." But it turned out to be a pretty good prediction because I did have to put out a fire. I mean I would have put it out if I could have gotten to it; but since none of us could get to it, I had to call the fire department.

One of Barry Stein's flares got stuck up in a tree and it just smoked and smoldered up there for a while, until a fire started. We tried putting a guy in the tree and then handing him up a garden hose, but the smoke kept driving him down. I called the fire department and opened a big gate so their truck could get onto the golf course. It never stopped play but the tree fire and firetruck drew quite a crowd.

As I was thanking the firemen for putting out the fire, Bobby Sanchez hit a very long, but not very straight, two-hundred-yard two iron that hit the fireman I was talking to in the back. He was still pretty mad when Bobby showed up in his golf cart and said he was sorry. When the fireman saw Viva Zapata, his entire mood changed and he said to Bobby, "Oh, it wasn't nothing."

It took the firetruck a lot longer to get off the golf course than it did to get on because, every time the firemen took one of the inner-city kids off the truck, three more would jump on. Marcella Mississippi drove a golf cart out to get the kids. About thirty of them were in, on top of, and hanging off the side of that cart. Marcella yelled, "Hi, Dale!" as she drove by me with all of those kids.

All those kids fell in love with Marcella and she, more than anyone, was responsible for getting them off the course. She got them back to the clubhouse area where she entertained them all by singing with Big Shrimpy and The Crabs.

Play was still slow and it was even slower than the planners thought it would be. One of the reasons the tournament took so long to play was "The Heckle Hole." Some of the comedians took it upon themselves to designate the eighteenth hole as "The Heckle Hole." They didn't run their idea by the board of directors. They just took a big portable blackboard out of the meeting room of the clubhouse, wrote "The Heckle Hole" on it and put it on the eighteenth tee box.

They heckled people from the tee box, all the way up the eighteenth fairway to the green that was in front of the clubhouse and first tee.

The first heckle I heard was when Bob Wurley, the representative from the sportswear company, was on the eighteenth tee box and at the top of his back swing, one of the comics said, "Hey, Bob, your wife called and I took the message. She's leaving you for the Houston Rockets."

Bob actually stopped his swing and looked around which prompted another one of the comics to say, "Speaking of your wife, does she know you're wearing one of her outfits?"

Bob Wurley didn't say anything but he did look shocked. I admired the fact that he got back over the ball and took a big swing, but he hit a ground ball that only went about fifty yards. He cussed all the way to his ball and the comics walked with him saying things like, "This ain't bowling, Bob! You're not supposed to roll the ball!"

It was a morbid fascination for me—I could not resist hanging around the eighteenth hole and watching the comics heckle the players. The comedians didn't bother heckling any of their fellow comics because they were used to being heckled. But they loved heckling "the civilians" and a lot of their comments had to do with the players' golf swings.

"Your swing looks like a cross between Arnold Palmer and Arnold, that pig on *Green Acres.*"

"The last time I saw a swing like that I was watching a man have an epileptic fit!"

"A blindfolded kid swinging a broomstick at a *piñata* looks better than your golf swing!"

What the comics went for next always seemed to be the player's clothing.

"Where'd you find the golf hat? In a box of cereal?"

"Somebody call Liberace and tell him I just located his visor!"

"I don't want to say that your outfit is loud, but would you mind turning it down? I can't hear Big Shrimpy and The Crabs!"

"The only thing louder than your outfit is my first wife!"

Alex Lewis said to a very large man who was representing a car dealership, "What do you do with that golf shirt when you're not wearing it? Use it as a car cover? That's not a shirt—that's an awning! Families should be picnicking under that thing!"

Another comic said of that man's very large golf shoes, "The last time I saw something that big that had spikes in it, I was mining a harbor with the Navy Seals!"

When the foursome that included Bobby Ray Sutton and Dr. Walter Kellogg came to the eighteenth tee, someone commented that they looked like "typical country club Republicans with their white shoes and matching belts." That prompted Steven Reed to act like an announcer and yell, "Ladies and gentlemen! The stars of the movie, *Young Republicans From Hell*! Starring Bobby Ray Sutton as the phony two-faced golf pro who competes in tournaments for charity by day, and by night performs as Tina Turner in a drag queen review at the local gay bar! And Dr. Walter Kellogg! The respected head of a children's hospital by day and by night he becomes Judy Garland in the same drag queen review with Bobby Ray Sutton! Maybe we can get the good doctor to sing, 'Somewhere Over the Rainbow' after he tees off!"

Lance Childress of *Good Morning, Houston* was wearing a yellow golf shirt with red trim. It prompted one comic to comment, "Hey, Lance! I didn't know McDonald's made a line of golf shirts! Did you get an order of fries with that shirt? By the way, does Ronald McDonald know you are wearing his pants?"

Lance didn't say anything but he did start to chase one of those comedians. I watched them run the length of the eighteenth fairway, and then the comic disappeared into the crowd at the clubhouse. I could see Lance standing in front of the band looking around as Marcella Mississippi sang the Aretha Franklin hit, "Respect."

The comedians were equal opportunity on The Heckle Hole and were just as tough on the women as they were on the men. "You women have no business being out here! You should be home cooking, cleaning, working on new recipes! No, we're just kidding, ladies. We believe in women's rights. We believe a woman has the right to do whatever a man tells her to do!"

Bonnie Praline was the biggest target of the comedians and she threw a ball at one of them after he said,

"What size shoe is that you're wearing, Bonnie? I didn't know that Goodyear was making a golf shoe!"

I saw her sobbing on the eighteenth green when one of the comics asked her, "Excuse me. Didn't you star in the movie, *Attack of the Killer Thighs?*"

Other than Bonnie Praline's sobbing and her partner Lance Childress chasing that comic the length of the eighteenth fairway, there really wasn't any bad blood during the tournament. Billy Meyer fought two different guys who propositioned Edna "Too Tall" Jones, but I figured Billy getting into fights was like all those people getting hit by stray golf balls—it just had to happen.

I took another little walk around the golf course and thought about how I didn't want the day to end. I knew that the end of the day would mark the beginning of the end for The Comedy Werks and maybe Houston comedy in general. All of the repercussions would start tomorrow. Everyone would know that businesses were abused and lied to, as were many charities. Sergeant Harry Herndon's investigation would start showing up in the newspaper and the Alcohol Control people would go after The Comedy Werks.

At that moment I noticed Sergeant Herndon, who looked like a lion that just spotted his prey. He was all perked up and his body looked coiled like he was ready to strike. I saw what Herndon was staring at and I couldn't believe that Packy Hester would make such a dumb mistake. He had just passed something, probably a vial, to a bartender from The Laff A Lot and I saw it from twenty yards away. I kept walking in that direction. What I heard from fifteen yards away was Jimmy Clark, who said to the bartender and Packy, "Give me a toot, man!"

I watched the gears churning in Sergeant Herndon's head. The bartender was now holding the vial so maybe Packy wasn't holding anything. Sergeant Herndon wanted Packy so bad he could hardly stand it, and he knew that the best way to get him was through the alcohol soaked, drugged-out Jimmy Clark. Jimmy finally went to the public restroom to smoke a joint and it was there he was busted by Sergeant Herndon. It took Jimmy about ten seconds to give up Packy.

I followed closely and heard Sergeant Herndon inform Packy he was under arrest. He then read him his rights as he handcuffed him to the door handle of his car. There was one hundred and fifty dollars in Packy's right front pocket, and Packy had made another slip when he left two amphetamine tablets in his left front pocket.

It was like an Easter egg hunt for Herndon as he excitedly went through Packy's car. He found one purse-sized bag that had about seven Baggies of marijuana in it and another bag that had some vials of crystal Methedrine, and a jar with capsules in it. Harry told Packy not to even try to help him by telling him where everything was, because he wasn't going to make it any easier on him no matter how much he cooperated.

I didn't want to startle the sergeant and I knew how far away to stand when a policeman is working. My dad taught me years ago that it wasn't a good idea to walk up on a police officer while he was arresting someone. It was a good way to get yourself hurt or arrested. I felt that I was standing far enough away as I said in a fairly soft voice, "What do you have, Sergeant?"

"It's all mine!" a startled Harry exclaimed just like a selfish child. "I've worked this whole tournament, ever since the beginning! I knew it was dirty from day one and I've got it all documented. And now this—drugs! And a lot of them!"

"Congratulations, Sergeant," I said in a positive tone. "I hate drugs."

Herndon snuck a glance at me and said, "You sure hang out with enough dopers for someone who hates drugs."

He added, "You better find a new place to tell your jokes because I'm taking down The Comedy Werks and not even your father could stop me. Even if I never found this drug dealer, I was going to the newspapers with everything those scum bag comedians and club owners have done. I've documented it all. Procuring goods and services for themselves in the name of Children's Charities. Just this morning I've got some of them for trespassing and destruction of property on this golf course. Allowing those kids to run around on the golf course, that's child endangerment! Drug dealers! Topless dancers! This thing should have been called The Degenerates Open!"

Sergeant Herndon went back to his search and after quickly looking through a combination phone and appointment book, he threw it behind him. It landed almost at my feet. I picked it up and soon became very interested in it. Herndon never would have noticed it, because he was obsessed with looking for the money and the drugs. I knew that I was onto something with the phone book with the literally hundreds of phone numbers with area codes from all over southern Texas. I finally said to Packy, "You're a mule for the Garcia brothers, aren't you?"

Packy just looked down at his feet and I kept looking through the book and I also found what appeared to be telephone credit card numbers. Harry found five hundred more dollars and some grams of cocaine. Harry was so excited he was frothing at the mouth and the veins in his forehead were popping out. An idea slowly started to come to me and although I didn't show it, I slowly started to get as excited as Harry Herndon was. When I got my idea formulated in my head, I knew that the only bad part of it was Sergeant Herndon probably wouldn't even listen to it. I knew that I had to try, so I went real slow and careful with him.

"Sergeant," I began. "I want to learn something, so tell me when I'm wrong here."

Herndon went along with me by saying, "Okay, shoot," but he kept his search going.

I went on, "You've got this guy good, there's no doubt about it. You got him legal and you got him pinned to the wall."

"Right so far," said Harry as he kept looking.

I continued, "Something else that I'm almost just as sure of is that this guy works for the Garcia brothers and he wouldn't roll over on the Garcia brothers for any kind of deal, because he knows if he does, he's dead. So what we've got is a guy with drugs and drug money who's going to go away for a long time. But nothing is going to happen to the Garcia brothers, who will just keep on doing what they are doing, but it's still a good bust and you'll look good with the department and you might even get your name in the paper."

The sergeant didn't respond immediately, but he finally said, "That sounds about right and it sounds good to me."

"I've got an idea, Sergeant," I said calmly. "And all that I ask is that you hear me out before you go crazy." Harry didn't look at me and he didn't say anything either. I then looked at Packy and asked, "How would you like not to go to prison for drug trafficking?"

The first time I verbalized my plan, Sergeant Herndon did, in fact, go crazy and his basic message was "I don't give a damn who your father is! I'll take you to jail!" I had to ignore him for a moment as I said to Packy, "How much cash money can the Garcia brothers raise between now and the show tonight?"

Sergeant Herndon said forcefully, "That's enough, Chase."

I just kept looking at Packy as I asked, "Twenty-five thousand?" I knew he wasn't going to answer me but I was hoping his face would give me the answer. When I said twenty-five thousand Packy looked like he was going to burst out laughing.

Sergeant Herndon was a little louder as he warned, "You keep this shit up, you'll be going to jail too."

"How about fifty thousand, Packy?" I asked and he didn't flinch. "Can they go seventy-five thousand?"

"Chase!" Sergeant Herndon screamed at me.

I didn't figure I had anything to lose, but I didn't want to get arrested either. I looked at Sergeant Herndon and said, "I have to ask him one last question." I looked at Packy and said, "Can the Garcia brothers go six figures?"

Sergeant Herndon screamed, "One more question and I'll handcuff you to this punk!"

It took about a minute for things to calm down enough for me to lay my plan out to the sergeant. I explained the wonderful ramifications it had for the community and that the guilty would still be punished, including the Garcia brothers. Convincing the sergeant was like peeling the layers off an onion, but ever so slowly he started to listen.

He finally started to come around, especially when I explained to him, "It's perfect, because if my way doesn't work, then we go right back to your way." He didn't argue with that and, even though he kept swearing, he finally let me try.

CHAPTER TWELVE

Sergeant Herndon was still not completely sold on my idea, but Packy was and Packy even dialed the phone number for me. We were at a phone booth not far from Packy's car. Packy got one of the Garcia brothers on the phone and explained he had been busted and was with a sergeant with the Houston Police Department and I cringed when he said, "and the son of the chief of police." Packy then said I had an idea that was good for everybody involved. He then put me on the line.

"Hi, this is Dale Chase and I'm here with a police sergeant and you don't have to say anything but be sure you listen closely. Packy Hester is under arrest for drug sales and trafficking. The sergeant got him with two thousand dollars in cash and a lot of drugs. We also know that he works for you guys, but we could never prove that because Packy would never testify against you guys. But I think we have some things that could cause you a lot of problems in the press. I'm talking bad publicity for your businesses. Packy has a book with about five hundred first names in it, with phone numbers and area codes all over southern Texas, all the places you guys got bars. The sergeant also has Packy very large in the felony department in telephone fraud, as in using other people's phone credit cards. Now, whoever I am talking to, listen closely, because I am only going to say this once and I don't want to hear you say 'What?' As a matter of fact, I don't want to hear you say anything."

I took a breath and looked at Sergeant Herndon who was handcuffed to Packy. I talked calmly yet authoritatively into the phone. "If you do what I tell you, Packy is not going to be charged with any drug offense, not trafficking, sales, or even possession. He will be charged with telephone credit card fraud and you will help him out with a lawyer, of course, and pay his fine. The drugs the sergeant confiscated will be destroyed, but we will keep the money and give it to charity. We are right now at The Comics Open charity golf tournament at El Rancho Heights Golf Course. We are on our way to El Rancho Heights High School where there will be a charity comedy show starting at seven and going until about ten. At some time during that show, a representative of yours will show up at the auditorium and give the sergeant a bag with one hundred thousand dollars cash in it for charity. If that happens, Packy is charged with credit card fraud only. If no one shows up with a bag with one hundred thousand dollars in it, then Packy is charged with drug trafficking and we start calling all of your customers in that telephone book. And you will also start hearing about the Garcia brothers on the television a lot and in the newspapers. What happens is totally up to you.

"Your representative can ask for me because everybody knows me, or they can find the sergeant standing by the side door next to the stage. He is wearing a bright yellow Hawaiian print shirt with matching shorts and brown socks and sandals. Packy will be with us. What happens is totally up to you." With that, I hung up the phone.

CHAPTER THIRTEEN

People were slowly leaving the golf tournament and walking by the phone booth where Sergeant Herndon, Packy, and I were standing. Because of the passers-by we couldn't talk. That was just as well, because there was really nothing else to talk about. The three of us were looking at each other in wonderment. Packy and I were wondering if the plan would work and Sergeant Herndon was wondering why he was going along with it.

We had my plan and, if that didn't work, we would go back and do it Sergeant Herndon's way. Packy and I were rooting desperately for my plan to work and I knew, in his heart of hearts, so was Harry Herndon.

Most of the players, including the comics, sponsors, volunteers, and even the crowd, went directly from the golf tournament over to the show. The auditorium was filling up fast, and Sergeant Herndon quietly and without fanfare handcuffed Packy to a chair in the front row closest to the exit. I didn't sit down much and neither did Harry. Harry kept standing by the side door, looking at the parking lot, and Packy kept looking at Harry, hoping he would see something.

The show actually started at about six forty-five and it did not start the way they had planned it. While everyone was being seated, some taped music was played over the sound system and then a musician from The Laff Inn came out and played a piano that was onstage, off to the side. Reverend Witherspoon got the idea that his kids should go onstage and sing some songs, but Milt was against it. Marty then pointed out to his brother the three news cameras in the back of the auditorium and all of a sudden, Milt thought the children singing was a great idea.

It was very unexpected and the audience actually enjoyed it. Listening to all those kids sing was definitely better than staring at a closed curtain. Larry Lawrence got the idea that he and the Gay Men's Chorus of Houston, along with Linda Hart, should join the one hundred children onstage. Reverend Witherspoon, Milt, and Marty finally let them go on and they sang with the children "The Eyes of Texas." They all sang "The Rainbow Connection," and closed with the same song Jerry Lewis always sings to close his Labor Day telethon, "You'll Never Walk Alone." There wasn't a dry eye in The Gay Men's Chorus when they sang that song.

Milt told the comics backstage, "If anyone screws up this show with profanity or anything else, I will personally kill them. My brother and I are probably going to jail anyway, so I'll kill them and it won't make any difference. Anyway, enjoy the show."

The lights went down and "Proud Mary" came on, and as the curtain opened, an offstage announcer spoke into the sound system, "Please welcome the man who has been the driving force behind The Comics Open. Comedian and co-owner of The Comedy Werks and former grad of El Rancho Heights High School! Let's hear it for Milt Langley!"

The audience gave Milt a standing ovation that actually meant more to Marty than it did to his brother. Milt did a nice opening and got some big laughs. Then he had the volunteers, as well as the representatives from the golf course, stand to receive a round of applause. He had another round of applause for the children who sang before the show, as well as Linda Hart and what Milt described as "the men's chorus." He introduced Jackie and her court and, as they all stood and waved to the crowd, Jackie kept saying under her breath, "No tits, girls, no flashing of tits."

Marty had compiled a list from the comics of every business they had taken advantage of and he was going to have the emcee thank each and every one of those businesses a few at a time in between the acts. Milt introduced Bobby Ray Sutton, who also thanked some people. It looked like he was going to make some presentations that Milt and Marty had warned him against. Bobby Ray was told that no one in the audience cared who played the best round of golf at the tournament or who had the longest drive or closest to the pin. Bobby Ray disagreed, but his speech came to an immediate halt when Milt rolled the left wheel of his wheelchair up on to Bobby's foot.

The show actually started with a somewhat hokey but very effective musical number sung by Linda Hart. The taped music to the song "Make 'Em Laugh" played while Linda sang and, when the music stopped, some of the comics did a funny line or short sketch. The routine featured improvisational players from all of the Houston comedy clubs.

Bobby Sanchez did a sketch with Brent Harris where Bobby was looking off in the distance and he finally says to Brent, "I think it's a five iron."

Brent said back, "I'm not your caddy. It's bad enough caddying for the white man but I won't caddy for no Mexican."

"Lee Trevino's caddy is black," explained Bobby. "And if Trevino makes one million a year then his caddy makes at least a hundred thousand."

Brent thought for a moment and then said, "Yeah, I think it's a five iron." He then said to Greg Okada who was standing next to him, "Boy, go get me a five iron."

Milt introduced the first five comics who did straight standup for a maximum of seven minutes each. In between the acts, Milt thanked some more sponsors. That's how the entire show went, even after Milt turned the emcee chores over to Seth Harmon, one of the house emcees at Hilarities.

The highlight of the first five acts was the performance by Bill and Billy. They did an impression of the police helicopter going over The El Rancho Heights Golf Course describing what was going on at The Comics Open. Billy was sitting up on Big Bill's shoulders and Bill was holding the microphone up over his head so Billy could speak into it. Billy seemed to be maneuvering Bill by pulling on his ears. Billy was saying into the microphone, "We're up here in Police Chopper One over The Comics Open golf tournament! I see kids running everywhere! Flares! Smoke bombs! Two golf carts are in the lake! Is this a golf tournament or World War Three?"

My favorite part was when Bill and Billy were interrupted by Edna "Too Tall" Jones who yelled out from the third row, "That's my Billy! My Billy knows how to hang on to somebody's ears!"

I had told Milt and Marty I didn't want to perform on the show; but they must have thought I was kidding, because Marty informed me I'd be going on next "to cover all the celebrities that were promised to the people."

It was the only time I had ever been onstage and my mind was somewhere else. All I could think about was Sergeant Herndon, Packy, and the Garcia brothers. But I could hear laughter, especially from all the children, as I did Kermit the Frog, Miss Piggy, and Jerry Lewis.

I did my salute to cowboy musicals with impressions of Johnny Cash, Loretta Lynn, Willie Nelson, and "Willie's brother that he never talks about," played by Charles Nelson Reilly. I threw in a bunch of celebrities including Redd Foxx and Richard Nixon. I closed with Mick Jagger singing "Take Me Out to the Ballgame." The crowd was going crazy, but all I could think about was my father. My father, the chief of police, was standing in the back of the auditorium where I was trying to shake down some drug dealers for a hundred grand.

I could not sit down, so I leaned up against the wall next to the exit where Harry kept looking out into the parking lot. Milt was huddled up in that same area with his brother, Bobby Ray, Brenda, and a bookkeeper lady from The Laff A Lot who was in charge of keeping track of the proceeds for The Comics Open. The lady accountant informed them that a lot of the people who were at the show were comped in, like the children and all of the volunteers and members of the golf course. "We might do as high as five thousand on the show and that includes tickets, refreshments, and souvenirs. We're still counting the money from the tournament and money keeps trickling in from around the city and from that tape by Big Shrimpy and The Crabs. But the bottom line is, there is no avoiding the fact that we're going to be anywhere from ninety to one hundred grand short on what you've promised to charities."

Milt and Marty started talking about each of the club owners coming up with an extra five thousand but, besides being a very hard sell, it wouldn't come close to solving the problem. They ran the idea by Hank Bruno, the owner of The Comedy Corral, but his response was, "Shit fire! This thing has cost me enough! It was your idea, so why don't you cover the mistakes?"

Milt snapped at Hank, "Weren't you the one crying at the press conference about how you were going to lead the way in contributions?" Hank gave a very hard look to Milt, and Marty gave an even harder look to Hank.

I walked up the aisle past the door where Sergeant Herndon kept looking into the parking lot. I never once looked out that door. I figured if the Garcia brothers were sending someone, that person would definitely find us. If not, then I wasn't going to waste my time staring at the parking lot.

If the Garcia brothers were as smart as I thought they were, they would send the money. One hundred thousand was a number that would cause them a lot of pain and really piss them off, but that's what we wanted. It was also an amount of cash they could put together in a hurry. They had bars and nightclubs all over southern Texas and they could probably put that amount of money together without anyone even getting on an airplane. They would do it, I thought. They would chalk it up to "just the price of doing business."

Sergeant Herndon had finally gone along with the idea because I had really struck a nerve with him. I figured from what my dad had told me that guys like Harry Herndon were very idealistic when they became policemen, and really cared about doing good works and making the bad guys pay. But the really bad guys almost never paid, just guys the size of Packy Hester. The sergeant agreed that to do it the traditional way meant he would get some credit—Packy would go away. But the Garcia brothers would lose almost nothing. My idea would make the Garcia brothers pay, the sergeant would get credit for a big telephone credit card felony bust, and the children of Houston would benefit by over one hundred thousand dollars.

Sergeant Herndon liked the idea, but what he hated was that it required he set aside his hatred of The Comedy Werks. He was still unable to do that. He told me that he was still going to the papers with his story about how the comics got goods and services in the name of Children's Charities.

Although I was too preoccupied to really watch the show, I could tell by the laughter how much the crowd loved Barry Stein and his props. I did watch as Jake Davis and Marcus Pauley got the biggest laugh when they went onstage together and sang the Stevie Wonder/ Paul McCartney hit, "Ebony and Ivory."

But it was Marcella Mississippi who was the absolute hit of the show. The lighting was perfect for her grand entrance wearing her purple sequined gown. To all of the inner-city children she looked like an African queen. Her show was perfect, with children's nursery rhymes and stories that she had changed just a bit, injecting sexual innuendoes to make them fun for the adults as well. She also sang as Aretha Franklin, and everyone in the auditorium was clapping and swaying to the music. It was during Marcella's performance that the bag showed up.

A beautiful Hispanic woman came to the side door and I didn't notice her until Sergeant Herndon whispered, "Chase." She looked at me and I nodded. She looked at the sergeant's Hawaiian shirt and she even snuck a glance at Packy. She then said to me, "As I parked my car and was going to see the show, I found this bag laying in the parking lot. Can I leave it with you?"

The three of us knew she was the Garcia brothers' representative and I said, "How good of you. We'll take care of it from here."

Sergeant Herndon checked the money in the bag and added the two thousand, one hundred and forty-eight dollars he had taken off Packy. He then looked at me and said, "We've got to do it your way now."

I didn't explain anything to Milt and Marty—I just told them, "Trust me, introduce me next."

I was excited as well as nervous as I took the stage. The audience knew something was up because I had already performed. I grabbed the microphone with my right hand and said, "Ladies and gentlemen, I have something important to say and it involves telling you people the truth." I knew I got their attention with that statement so I continued. "I was there the night the idea for The Comics Open was born. I got to watch the original idea grow. And I saw the tremendous commitment from the comedians, comedy club owners, comedy club personnel, and most of all the people of Houston. It appeared to me and everyone else involved in this charity fund-raiser that we did everything right. We had organizational meetings, a board of directors, thousands of people donated their time, and sponsors lined up to donate their goods and services. And as hard as everyone worked—we came up way short on the monies, until just now."

The audience was dead silent and even the inner-city children were riding on my every word. I looked down at Milt and Marty and then took another look at my father standing in a doorway at the back of the auditorium. I went on, "It never occurred to me that The Comics Open would ever need saving, but it certainly has. We were saved from ourselves.

"Us comedians are a bunch of clowns who tried to do the right thing; but for every big step forward, we took two giant steps back. When the comedians heard what the fund-raising goal was, each one of them felt that they should raise that much money. Each comedian got as many sponsors as possible, promising each one an exclusive—and offending most of those sponsors in the process. The comedians promised far too many charities far too much money, but they didn't mean anything bad by it. They just wished that there was that much money to go around. And now, by a miracle there is."

I could feel the excitement rising in the auditorium. "We were saved by a man who isn't a clown. He is a public servant in the truest sense of the word. A man who answered a calling to serve his hometown of Houston, which he has done successfully for over twenty years."

I looked over at Harry Herndon and gestured at him as I said, "I want to introduce a man who, unlike the comedians, never gets any laughs and never hears a round of applause. I'm not sure he even gets the credit he deserves from the police department he works for. He is always behind the scenes. I just learned that today he personally broke a case of possibly the biggest telephone credit card fraud in the history of this state, or at least southern Texas. And all that time he also worked behind the scenes raising money for this tournament. Ladies and gentlemen, I now give you the man who saved The Comics Open! From the Houston Police Department, Sergeant Harry Herndon!"

Sergeant Herndon was in shock as the crowd roared and a spotlight spun over and shined down on him and his matching yellow Hawaiian outfit. Marty finally gestured for the waitress Patty to escort him to the stage. He walked up like a child clutching the bag of money. I saluted him and then shook his hand and pointed him to the microphone. The crowd went dead silent as Harry said into the microphone, "I have here a little over one hundred and two thousand dollars for the children of Houston."

The audience went absolutely berserk as pandemonium broke out in the auditorium. Harry's eyes were bugging out of his head as he watched a sea of humanity come rushing at him. Patty and then a horde of comedians hugged him. When Marcella got to him she gave him the biggest hug and a kiss right on the side of his head. Helen Scoggins, the president of Children's Charities of Houston, was sobbing as she hugged Harry.

Big Bill Blevens and Buddy Honeycutt hoisted Harry up on to their shoulders and then paraded him around the stage and the spotlight followed them. The spotlight stayed on them as Harry was taken down into the audience where he was mobbed by the inner-city children, the volunteers and most of the audience. The song "You'll Never Walk Alone" played over the sound system and again The Gay Men's Chorus sang and sobbed. Jackie and her court kept jumping up and down and they all made the biggest fuss over Harry.

As I stood off to the side of the stage watching all of the elation, my eyes caught Milt's and then Marty's. We had dodged a very big bullet. We looked at each other like we had survived a war and couldn't figure out why. I will always remember the way the three of us looked at each other.

I felt a presence and I knew who it was even before I turned around. My dad shook my hand and said, "Do I want to know what happened?"

I smiled and said, "My plan was based on a childhood memory. A memory that was played out in the headlights of your car one night."

Dad looked at me strangely as he tried to figure out what I was talking about. I went on. "My hero faced down two drug dealers and made them put their money and drugs on the hood of the car. You let them take their money back and after that you taught me about those drugs. Then we threw them away. You said it was a tradeoff, a kind of street justice. Well, in my plan we threw the drugs away but took their money and gave it to charity."

A smile came over his face as he finally remembered. Dad didn't say anything because his smile said it all. The crowd carrying Harry came by where we were standing and dad came to attention and saluted Sergeant Herndon. Harry's eyes bugged out even farther when he saw my dad saluting him.

The celebration went on for the longest time with everyone singing, screaming, and parading Harry Herndon around the auditorium. Harry's feet didn't touch the ground for about half an hour because he was up on Big Bill's and Buddy's shoulders that long. My feet didn't touch the ground until later that night because I was just that relieved.

It was the lead-in to all of the eleven o'clock Houston television news shows, with me saying, "The man who saved The Comics Open!" And Sergeant Herndon saying, "I have here a little over one hundred and two thousand dollars for the children of Houston." There were shots of the sergeant being carried around and being hugged and kissed. There was a closeup of Reverend Witherspoon saying into a camera, "Sergeant Harry Herndon is a miracle worker!"

I imagined that Harry's wife saw it all as she and her daughters were eating and watching the news. The daughters probably stopped eating for a moment and said simultaneously, "Isn't that Daddy?"

After the celebration, everyone left happy. Except Packy Hester, who wasn't exactly happy as Sergeant Herndon drove him to the station to book him on telephone credit card fraud. But at least he wasn't being booked for drug trafficking.

The sergeant and I had a nice talk in the parking lot before he left for the police station to book Packy. I told him, "I wasn't sure you would go for it, Sergeant."

"I wasn't sure I would either," he answered back. "I was so set on getting The Comedy Werks and those comics and now I'm not even sure why." He went on to say, "That was a great idea you had today. It was terrific street justice and all the bad people paid and the Children's Charities benefited. And I got to have my moment. I kept seeing those comics having their moment almost every night. Getting all that attention. Pretty girls and good-looking guys with great personalities, but not me. Not since I got a game-winning hit in little league and my dad saw me, and not since I got sworn in as a policeman in front of my family. I got to have a moment, Dale, and I thank you. I will never forget it."

I told him what I had learned from the whole thing. "It was a good idea but then everything got out of control. The line between right and wrong got blurred. It became an ordeal and we needed something extraordinary to save us. I learned a lot. I definitely learned a lesson." Harry gave me a nice smile and then he said he was going home. I said I was going to The Comedy Werks and I told him to "stop by if you have a chance."

Everyone who was at The Comedy Werks applauded me when I walked into the show room at about midnight. There was Milt, Marty, Brenda, Patty, and Carolyn. Clay was with Jackie and her court was there with Bobby, Brent, Greg, Barry Stein, Billy Meyer, and David Luben. There were some other comics and their dates and every-one was drinking and it was a mellow mood. Milt and Marty talked about "surviving the idea" and how "it went from a great idea to a nightmare to a dream come true."

At about one-fifteen that morning, Sergeant Harry Herndon walked into the show room and everyone, in-cluding the women, stood up. It was as though royalty had walked through the door, and in a way it had. Even Milt strained and pushed himself up on the hand rests of his wheelchair. Harry was still wearing his Hawaiian shirt with the matching shorts and brown socks and san-dals. No one said anything and Patty rushed over and got

Harry a beer and patted him on the back as she handed it to him.

Harry took a sip of his beer and everyone could see how good it tasted to him. He took another sip and he started to look different than he had every looked before, so relaxed—even his hair looked relaxed. At last Harry spoke, "And I wanted to close this place down."

Milt finally said, "We are putting up a sign over the bar that reads "Harry Herndon Drinks for Free." That same sign is going up in the other comedy clubs, too." Harry smiled and blushed a little bit as everyone said "Alright" and "Yeah, Harry!"

Milt said seriously to Harry, "We don't know how to thank you."

Harry looked at Milt and Marty and said, "My wife threw me out tonight. She saw it all on the news. Because of what happened tonight, because of you people, she is divorcing me."

The room fell completely silent and a few people said, "Oh, no." I could feel my entire body slump and I felt that terrible feeling in my stomach again. I looked around the room and everyone there looked as bad as I felt. I finally looked at Harry.

Harry then smiled a big beautiful smile and said, "So I came over to thank you. Thanks to all of you. Because of you people, I am free at last."

It was the biggest laugh Harry had ever gotten in his life. I had never felt that relieved—nor had anyone else in that show room. Harry sat on the stage and finished his beer and then had another. Patty sat next to him for a while and he couldn't hide how much he was enjoying the attention from everyone. Finally, Clay had something to say.

Clay stood up as he spoke. "Sergeant, it has been my honor to have been Queen Jackie's escort and bodyguard this week during the tournament and the show. She is a wonderful lady and she knows I'm leaving tomorrow on a five-week-long road trip to comedy clubs around this state and one in Oklahoma. I just asked her if there was one man I could introduce her to, who would that man be, and she said you. So Sergeant Harry Herndon, meet Jackie, 'The Golden Bear' Nicklaus."

It was a wonderful thing to have done. Clay, who was always the classiest of the comics, became even classier to everyone who was there. He sat Jackie on the stage next to Harry and then shook everyone's hand before he left. Milt followed him out to the parking lot where Marty and I joined them.

"That was cool," Marty said to Clay, and I concurred. Clay just smiled and said, "Who ever would have guessed that man would have ended up the MVP of the tournament. The least he deserved was to end up with the queen of the tournament."

Clay got into his car and started it up. As he pulled out of the parking lot we could hear him singing "On the Road Again."

As the three of us watched Clay's car disappear down the street, I said, "He was wrong, you know."

"Who was wrong?" Chimed Milt and Marty.

"George Orwell," I answered. "The guy who wrote that book *1984*. He wrote it in the 1940s, and he predicted that by 1984 everything and everybody would be controlled by computers and the government—even our thoughts. Brilliant man, that Orwell, but he never could have predicted the comedians. Maybe that is what we've learned from all of this. The comedians remind us that really nobody is in charge."

Marty looked at me and said sheepishly, "We'll never ask you where that money came from." Milt just shook his head and I just smiled.

Milt finally said, "We'll do it again next year. Next year it will be The Cops Open."

Marty added, "The cops and the son of the chief are better at raising money anyway."

I suddenly yawned and said, "Well, guys, I'm going home."

Milt said, "We're all sleeping in our own beds tonight. I thought we would all be sleeping together in a jail cell."

Milt and Marty then got the most sincere expressions on their faces and Milt said to me, "Thanks, Dale. I don't know all the details, and I don't need to, but thank you."

Marty added, "Everything is kind of a blur, Dale, but all I know for sure is that we want to thank you more than anybody."

Their words meant a lot to me but I just played it off with a "glad I could be a part of it."

I stood by my car and watched as Marty was pushing his brother in his wheelchair back toward the club. Milt said, "Marty, would you take that bag of golf clubs out of the utility closet? I don't want to see any more golf for a while."

Marty just answered, "Good idea, Milty." They rolled a little farther and then Marty asked, "I know it turned out to be quite a little bit more than we bargained for but, all things considered, did you have a good time?"

Milt laughed a small laugh as he answered, "I sure did, Marty. I sure did."

"Then so did I," added Marty. "Then so did I."

EPILOGUE

We were barely into the New Year when I started to hear the first murmurings about "the next Comics Open" and how "this one is going to be twice as big as the first one." I couldn't believe that everyone was ready to jump into another Comics Open after the first one had been such a complete disaster, only to be saved by a miracle.

Even Milt and Marty had forgotten about the pain and suffering they had been through because they now had a plaque. They had gotten what they always wanted when they went to city hall. In front of the city council, the mayor gave them a plaque for being "The Founders of The Comics Open." The mayor also referred to them as "two Houstonians of the highest order for spreading laughter and raising money for children's charities." Milt and Marty felt that their Comedy Werks had finally been legitimized into the hearts and minds of their fellow Houstonians.

But the two of them were deaf to me when I told them, "There's no such thing as controlling the comedians." Milt and Marty were also blind because they didn't even see the signs that the cycle was starting again. It was for a different reason this time (his fiancé had left him for another golf pro), but Bobby Ray Sutton showed up at The Comedy Werks at two thirty one morning, half-drunk and very depressed. The golf clubs came out again and soon golf balls were flying all over the show room. Jimmy Clark got his nose broken again.

Some of the comics were already wondering aloud what they had to do to get a car and two were overheard trying to finagle a free trip to Las Vegas to "scout celebrities for the next Comics Open." The waitress Patty described what was going on as "déjà vu all over again."

I was thinking of suggesting at the next organizational meeting that The Comics Open logo might be that statue of Lady Justice, the blindfolded woman who is holding out the scales of justice. The only difference would be that she would have a bag of golf clubs slung over her shoulder and she would be standing in front of a microphone stand. In her right hand, instead of a sword, she would be holding a crippled child, and in her left she would be holding the scales that were filled with money that the comedians had raised for the children's charities. The reason for her blindfold would be so she didn't have to see how the money was raised.

At the base of that statue would be cartoon caricatures of all the people who took part in the first Comic's Open—all the comics, club owners and club personnel. All of the comedians would be swinging golf clubs and wearing clothes with the price tags still on them and Clay and Harry Herndon would be standing next to a big-busted woman wearing a tiara. There would be a Lincoln Town Car packed with women and comics and a big pair of breasts would be sticking out of the side rear window.

My dad would be in that picture in his formal chief of police uniform and I would be standing next to him. I would be smiling and pointing in the opposite direction from the comedians. Trying my hardest to get my dad to look the other way.

THE END

ABOUT THE AUTHOR

For over twenty years Ron Kenney has been traveling the country performing in comedy clubs and playing golf. His pet peeves are a bad sound system and standing over his third putt. Ron lives in Santa Monica, California, just a chip shot from the beach. The Comics Open is his first novel.

Give the Gift of
The Comics Open
to Your Friends and Colleagues

CHECK YOUR LEADING BOOKSTORE OR ORDER HERE

❏ **YES**, I want ____ copies of *The Comics Open* at $9.95 each, plus $3 shipping per book (California residents please add $.82 sales tax per book). Canadian orders must be accompanied by a postal money order in U.S. funds. Allow 15 days for delivery.

My check or money order for $_____ is enclosed.
Please charge my: ❏ Visa   ❏ MasterCard
                             ❏ Discover   ❏ American Express

Name _____

Organization _____

Address _____

City/State/Zip _____

Phone_____   E-mail_____

Card # _____

Exp. Date_____   Signature _____

Please make your check payable and return to:
Samo Press, Inc.
2436 Fourth Street, #7
Santa Monica, CA 90405

Call your credit card order to: 310-396-5414